"THIS ... doorwa...

Bre... when she met his gaze, and she smiled. "I paid my light bill this month, I'm sure of it."

He glanced past her to her dimly lit shop. "Knowing that you tend to drag me into dark places, I thought I'd provide the lighting for our dinner."

"How thoughtful," she said casually as she invited him into the shop. "And to think most men settle for flowers or candy."

"No imagination."

"That's true," she said, turning to lead the way up the stairs to her apartment. "Although one man did bring his own silverware, which I thought was tacky." She made a startled sound when he wrapped his free arm around her waist and turned her to face him. "Now what's wrong?"

"I don't want to hear about other men you've been with." He left a trail of moist warmth as he touched his lips to her throat, the corner of her mouth, her cheek. Against her mouth, he said, "I don't want anyone touching you but me. . . ."

WHAT ARE *LOVESWEPT* ROMANCES?

They are stories of true romance and touching emotion. We believe those two very important ingredients are constants in our highly sensual and very believable stories in the LOVE-SWEPT line. Our goal is to give you, the reader, stories of consistently high quality that may sometimes make you laugh, sometimes make you cry, but are always fresh and creative and contain many delightful surprises within their pages.

Most romance fans read an enormous number of books. Those they truly love, they keep. Others may be traded with friends and soon forgotten. We hope that each LOVESWEPT romance will be a treasure—a "keeper." We will always try to publish

LOVE STORIES YOU'LL NEVER FORGET
BY AUTHORS YOU'LL ALWAYS REMEMBER

The Editors

Loveswept ®728

HOT SOUTHERN NIGHTS

PATT BUCHEISTER

BANTAM BOOKS
NEW YORK · TORONTO · LONDON · SYDNEY · AUCKLAND

HOT SOUTHERN NIGHTS
A Bantam Book / February 1995

If you would be interested in receiving protective vinyl covers for your
Loveswept books, please write to this address for information:

Loveswept
Bantam Books
P.O. Box 985
Hicksville, NY 11802

ISBN 0-553-44497-2

Published simultaneously in the United States and Canada

Bantam Books are published by Bantam Books, a division of Bantam Doubleday Dell Publishing Group, Inc. Its trademark, consisting of the words
"Bantam Books" and the portrayal of a rooster, is Registered in U.S. Patent
and Trademark Office and in other countries. Marca Registrada. Bantam
Books, 1540 Broadway, New York, New York 10036.

PRINTED IN THE UNITED STATES OF AMERICA

OPM   0 9 8 7 6 5 4 3 2 1

AUTHOR'S NOTE

With the advent of grandchildren into my life, I have become re-acquainted with the wondrous world of fairy tales and nursery rhymes. After re-reading the story of *Little Red Riding Hood* recently, I had the idea of writing a romance about a red-haired woman with a red hooded coat who lived in her great-great-great-grandmother's ancestral house. The hero would, of course, be the cranky wolf who eventually would forsake his bad habits and become the love of her life.

In the process of putting that terribly clever brainstorm on paper, I took a day off to attend the one-hundred-and-thirty-year anniversary tour of the Civil War battle of North Anna near Richmond, Virginia. (My husband and I are members of the Roanoke Chapter of the Civil War Roundtable and the Association for the Preservation of Civil War Battlefields.) While walking over the same ground where many of our ancestors had fought and lost their lives, I decided it would be interesting to drop a few names and places from a popular Civil War romance into my modern-day fairy tale.

So come with me into a story that will provide a feast for chocolate lovers and Civil War buffs, along with the story of two people who learn the magic of *Hot Southern Nights*.

Patt Bucheister

ONE

Like a baby taking his first steps, filming a documentary sometimes stumbled along for a while before it finally hit its stride. Director Sam Horne knew from experience that even a small film was likely to have moments when nothing ran smoothly. The large-scale one he was finishing up in northern Virginia—the longest documentary of his career, a four-hour film on the battle of Fredericksburg during the Civil War—had already taken six months of planning, writing, rewriting, taping, and negotiating.

On the day he was scheduled to shoot some simple background shots, nothing was running, walking, or even crawling.

What frustrated him even more was knowing that shooting the most dramatic part of the film would be stalled if he couldn't get a certain stubborn lady to cooperate with him. He wanted to use her plantation home as the setting for the encampments of the Confederate and Union armies—which would be played by experienced reenactors—and as the makeshift hospital for treating wounded Confederate soldiers. Until he got her signature on a lease agreement, he had to make do with fill-in shots.

It was like settling for an appetizer when he wanted to get down to the meat and potatoes.

Every time Sam complained about the delay to his business partner and producer, Darren Fentress, Darren told him he was too used to having his own way. Sam was honest enough with himself and with Darren to admit there was some truth in what his friend said. By nature, Sam didn't settle for second best. There was Sam's way and the right way. In his mind, they were the same thing.

His drive for the best in everything, from script to the most talented actors, had been partly responsible for the awards he'd won since his first film went public when he was twenty-eight. Now, ten years later, with an Emmy topping off his successes, he had the clout to get anything he wanted in order to make a film.

He wanted Maddox Hill Plantation.

Finding private land that could be filmed from any angle without evidence of the twentieth century was extremely difficult. At Maddox Hill, power and phone lines were underground, and aside from the modern vehicles belonging to visitors and the staff, the house and grounds would photograph beautifully, as if it were actually the nineteenth century.

Maddox Hill Plantation met every one of his requirements: space, location, ambience, appropriate terrain, and historical significance. In other words, it was perfect. Sam loved perfection.

His desire for perfection was coupled with an ability to visualize every scene he wanted to film down to the smallest detail. His innate curiosity was also behind his insistence that every fact be checked twice, then scrutinized again. Sam was considered brilliant by his contemporaries and even by his competitors, and was well liked and respected by his crew. He never asked anyone to work harder or longer than he did himself.

Patience, however, was not one of his finer attributes. He didn't expect every little thing to go smoothly every second. But he did expect them at least to go.

This particular day was turning into one that would try the patience of a saint. Not even his mother would call Sam Horne a saint.

His crew had set up to do some filming in Fredericksburg, but the only thing they'd accomplished was to push Sam's level of tolerance over the edge as there was one delay after the other. The weather was part of the problem. Although the battle of Fredericksburg had taken place the thirteenth of December in 1862, Sam needed every day in November with decent lighting he could get if he was going to stay on schedule. The lighting this day had been erratic at best.

From his position next to the main camera, Sam glanced up at the sky and scowled at the dark clouds rapidly filling it. Mother Nature wasn't co-operating.

Another woman, he groused silently. It figured.

Instead of having three hours of light left to work with, it looked like he had maybe thirty minutes before the sunlight would be replaced entirely by overcast skies.

Pure unadulterated stubbornness kept Sam from ordering the crew to pack it in. After all, the actors and the production crew were all getting paid for a full day's work. He wanted at least a few minutes of film to show for it.

His original plan when he'd set out from the hotel that morning had been to film various background shots depicting the Civil War era. At the moment two male actors and one female actor dressed in mid-nineteenth-century costumes were positioned in front of the Hugh Mercer Apothecary Shop in the picturesque Old Town section of Fredericksburg. Sam had planned to move down the street to include F. Kennedy's Mill House, but they wouldn't have enough time now.

Setting up a shot in public had its drawbacks, mainly curious onlookers and the occasional sidewalk critic who had a suggestion or two to make. Due to a bureaucratic mix-up with a city permit, the police hadn't been allowed to eliminate vehicle traffic completely from the intersection of Caroline and Amelia streets until an hour ago. Pedestrians were controlled by wooden barriers and polite but firm warning signs, reinforced by private security guards at certain key places, but it had been a difficult challenge to prohibit both foot and vehicular traffic on the brick streets.

Old Town Fredericksburg with its quaint specialty shops was popular at any time of the year. The cool November air didn't discourage the career shopaholic or the avid tourist who was determined not to miss a single attraction. Civil War scholars and students of all ages flocked to the battleground outside of town every day of the year and ventured into Old Town as part of their visit.

The sights of Fredericksburg, though, couldn't compete with a film crew at work.

Sam was aware of the crowds gathered behind the barriers, but he wasn't intimidated by their presence. Most of the time he ignored them. Like the technical problems and delays that inevitably cropped up when filming, Sam accepted the audience as part of the business of making documentary films—as long as they didn't interfere.

He turned to Darren, who as usual was standing nearby. The tall New Yorker was Sam's right hand, his sounding board, his trusted adviser, and on occasion his conscience.

"Don't say it," Sam muttered.

"Who me?" Darren put one hand on his chest, pretending to be mortally wounded. "I'm not the sort of person to continually remind you that we would be able to film the good stuff first if you had consented to have a backup location if Maddox Hill didn't work out."

"I'm so glad you're above that type of petty behavior, Darren. You might get your way yet if I can't convince Miss Southern to let us use her plantation."

"Which would be another delay while we start all over searching for another location. Why don't you just take hundred-dollar bills and throw them up in the air? It will be faster."

"Let's play filmmaker instead and get what we can before the light disappears completely."

Looking past Sam, Darren drawled, "Unless you plan on rewriting history by having Little Red Riding Hood involved in the War Between the States, you might want to hold off for a few more minutes."

Sam grinned. "You shouldn't have had all that coffee with your sandwich for lunch. The caffeine's rotted your brain cells. Red Riding Hood wasn't at the battle of Fredericksburg."

"Maybe not, but she's making an appearance in your shot." Darren jerked his head at something to Sam's right. "See for yourself. She just sneaked through the barrier with a basket of goodies to take to Grandma's house."

Humoring his friend, Sam glanced around, then did a double take. A woman carrying a white wicker basket was casually walking along the brick street, directly in front of the costumed actors. She was wearing a bright red jacket that fell to midthigh and had a folded hood lying on the back of her shoulders.

If the woman noticed that the clothes worn by the three people near the apothecary shop were about a hundred years out of date, she didn't appear to think they were unusual. She glanced their way, then returned her attention to the street in front of her.

"Hey, lady!" Sam yelled at her. "Take a different route to Grandma's house. You're in the way."

She obviously heard him. Anyone within a block radius would have. Sam's deep voice had a resonance that carried a fair distance without the aid of a loudspeaker.

The woman in the red hooded coat looked in his direction, her glance brushing over Sam and the five other men clustered beside the camera aimed at the shop. She either didn't think the peculiar shouted message had been directed at her, or she didn't care. She kept walking.

"Dammit, Red! Where the hell do you think you're going?"

He had been referring to the jacket she wore, but she apparently had heard the nickname before for a different reason. As she turned her head toward him again the bright lights from one of the panels aimed at the actors glinted in the auburn strands that brightened her brown hair.

She stopped and glared at him. "Are you yelling at me?"

He clamped his hands on his hips. "Do you see anybody else who's blocking our shot?"

Her gaze shifted to the camera, then around to the trio in period costume. Bringing her gaze back to slam into his, she said, "So take your picture. I'm not in the line of fire."

"It's a wide-angle lens. Trust me, you're in the shot. Move sometime today, Red. We're not getting any younger, and daylight, what there is of it, is fading fast."

"The last time I read the paper, this was still a free country. Save your Big Bad Wolf act for someone else."

Sam's mouth quirked at her retort, although humor wasn't the emotion he was trying to get across to the woman. His amusement deepened when he saw her stiffen as she caught a glimpse of his mocking smile.

She gave him a blistering look that would have singed his skin if he had been standing closer. Lifting her chin defiantly, she started walking again to the other side of the street, ignoring him once more.

Unfortunately, the route she chose meant she would still be in the way of filming.

Sam's hands on his hips became fists as he glared at her. "Red, you're really beginning to annoy me. What do you think you're doing?"

Giving him a cool look over her shoulder, she said casually, "I believe it's called walking."

"Cute. Real cute," he snapped. "Now get your sweet little tush out of the way."

She bristled like a cat. "I'm not in your way, and leave my tush out of this."

"The hell you aren't," he growled. The frustrations of the day and the disappointing results of his last phone conversation with a local lawyer centered on the only outlet he had at the moment. Her.

"Can't you see we're trying to film a scene here? Can't you go around us?"

She stopped walking again and gestured with her hand as she spoke with exaggerated patience, as though he were brain-dead. "I'm here. My car is over there. The shortest distance between those two points is where I'm walking. If you would stop yelling at me, I will march my sweet little tush to my car and drive away."

"Dammit, Red! We're losing the light."

She looked down an exquisitely shaped nose and drawled, "You're losing your mind."

Sam heard Darren chuckle and gave his partner a quelling glance that only made Darren laugh outright. Sam jerked his head around to the woman, more determined than ever to accomplish something that day. Even if it was just to get rid of the nuisance the woman had become.

When he turned to look at her again, he was just in time to see her trip on one of the thick cables strung across the intersection to the panel of lights.

Sam was moving before he even thought about it. He was only a couple of feet away from her when she lost her balance and went down onto one knee. The basket fell out of her hand, some of its contents spilling onto the brick street. Asphalt was nasty enough to fall on. The rough edges of the bricks could do much more damage to soft skin.

And her skin looked especially soft, he noted.

"Are you all right?" he asked as he bent over her.

"I've had more fun at the dentist," she grumbled. She examined her knee. The skin was scratched and raw in a patch the size of a walnut. "Aside from needing a new pair of panty hose, I'll live. Go back to your picture taking. I should be out of range by now. I'll just crawl away."

Sam reached for her arm and became even more irritated with her when she pulled away from him.

"Don't be so damn stubborn, Red. Let me help you up."

She shook her head. "I need to pick up the stuff that spilled out when I fell. If it will ease your conscience, you can help me gather everything back into the basket."

It took a lot to surprise Sam, but this woman managed to accomplish that feat with remarkable ease. "Lady, you must have bumped your head when you fell. I don't feel one bit guilty about you falling, because it wasn't my fault. You weren't watching where you were going, which seems to be your usual operating procedure."

"I've walked across this street hundreds of times. Cables and wires aren't usually part of it. Correct me if I'm wrong, but don't they belong to you?"

Sam wasn't paying that much attention to what she was saying. For some ridiculous reason, he was staring at her lips, fascinated by the way they moved to form her words. What he considered really dumb was that he was wondering how those lips would taste.

Giving himself a mental shake, he muttered, "Perhaps if we put flashing neon lights on the cables, you might see them next time."

Brett Southern smiled as she watched the bad-tempered, dark-haired man bend down and reach for a small plastic item near his foot. The baby rattle looked tiny in comparison with his large masculine hand. But then, he was a rather impressive man altogether, she reflected. He also had the ego to go with his size, considering he gave orders like a drill sergeant and expected to be instantly obeyed.

She set the basket upright and began piling the contents back into it. As she replaced them she was relieved to see that the only item in need of repair was her panty hose. All the candy lollipops had somehow survived. Even the blue-and-pink ribbon was still tied to the basket's handle in its complicated bow.

Once every item had been retrieved, Brett stood up. The man did too. He held a small container of baby powder in his hand, but he didn't immediately give it to her. He was looking at her with a strange expression on his face.

She felt her breath catch in her throat as she met his intense gaze. She'd never seen eyes quite like his before. They were a light brown, like doeskin. The color of his eyes was the only feature of his that could qualify as being soft, however. The way he held his head and lean body reminded her more of a proud stag accustomed to authority, ready to challenge anything or anyone that might have the nerve to cross his path.

Growing uncomfortable under his stare, she lifted her chin. "Are you going to give me that baby powder or do you need it?"

He blinked, shook his head, and handed her the container. "When's the baby due?"

She gaped at him. "What baby?"

He jerked his head toward the basket looped over her arm, brimming once again with pink and blue baby items, then in the general vicinity of her stomach, which was covered by her red jacket.

Frowning, he said, "Maybe you should get checked out by your doctor. You might have jarred something loose when you fell."

Good Lord, he thought she was pregnant. She bit her bottom lip to keep from laughing out loud.

When she'd left her shop a few minutes ago, she'd wanted something to take her mind off her meeting later with her attorney. She'd gotten her wish. The man who'd started yelling at her from the moment she'd stepped off the curb was providing entertainment of a sort, even though she was sure that wasn't his intention.

"Nothing was damaged, bruised, or jarred loose," she said soothingly. "You don't need to worry that I'll sue you."

"Sue me?" he exploded. "Lady, you are certifiable. It wasn't my fault you weren't watching where you were going."

The voice of reason interjected from a few feet behind him, calling Sam's name. Turning, Sam saw Darren was struggling to keep a straight face.

"If we're going to get anything on film today, we'd better get to it, Sam. Those clouds are really rolling in. We have maybe ten, fifteen minutes left of decent light."

"Yeah. Okay," he said grudgingly. "I'll be right there."

Sam turned back to the woman who'd been the cause of the latest delay, but she hadn't waited for him to continue yelling at her.

He caught a glimpse of the sleeve of her red jacket as she closed the door of her car. Feeling ridiculous, he wondered why he was so disappointed that she was leaving. She was out of the way, which was what he'd been harping on for the last five minutes.

He stared after her car as she expertly maneuvered the small compact out of its parking space and drove away. It was odd how he remembered little details about her he hadn't realized he'd noticed. Like the glint of mischief in her green eyes, the small mole just below the outer corner of her left eye, the way the lights had gleamed in the auburn strands, making them appear like fiery threads of flame woven through her luscious brown hair.

"Maybe it's something in the water," Darren murmured.

Sam didn't have to ask what his friend meant. They spoke in the verbal shorthand of old friends who knew each other well.

"The women around here do seem to have minds of their own, don't they?" Sam said. "Do you suppose that's typical of all southern women, or are we just running into the pick of the litter? First Miss Southern of Maddox Hill Plantation, now Little Red Riding Rude."

"Beats me," Darren drawled, falling into step beside Sam as he walked back to the camera.

"I know one particular southern woman," Sam continued, "who is going to put a major crimp in our plans unless we can persuade her to give us permission to use her land. Miss Southern's been a royal pain ever since we first contacted her."

Darren glanced at his watch. "Which reminds me. Don't forget you have an appointment at her lawyer's office in an hour. It's only about four blocks from here, so we can go ahead with this shot before you have to hustle over there and charm the stubborn woman into signing the releases."

Sam spoke to the man waiting behind the camera. "Go ahead, Hank. Get the shot of the group in front of the apothecary shop before we have Little Miss Muffet trotting in front of the camera next." Nodding to the cameraman, he said, "Let's do it."

This time no one interfered. The actors did their parts perfectly on the first take and the sunlight held. The camera scanned the area in front of the shop and the three actors from two different angles. A minute after Sam was satisfied they had caught enough to work with, the clouds blocked out the sun. The timing couldn't have been better.

Sam's mood had improved vastly by the time he left Darren in charge of the crew packing up the equipment. He would meet them all back at the hotel, hopefully with the news that they had finally gotten the necessary permission to use Maddox Hill Plantation.

His staff had researched a number of properties in Virginia, but none of them met all the requirements better than Maddox Hill, which had the added bonus of being close to Fredericksburg. They would have to commute longer distances every day if an alternative site had to be used.

Sam and some of his crew had visited Maddox Hill when they arrived in Virginia, and had taken the guided tour of the home. After seeing the plantation, and after meeting many of the reenactors he would be using, Sam knew the crucial battle scenes and hospital scenes were going to be better than he had hoped.

The only person standing in the way was the Southern woman.

Since he had a little time to spare, Sam walked the four blocks to the lawyer's office instead of driving his rental car. He used the opportunity to think about how to approach the woman. Her previous refusals had been blunt and without apology, accompanied by only the simple explanation that she didn't want her land used for commercial purposes. Sam and Darren considered that explanation pure hogwash. After all, she allowed the place to be open to the public for tours. There was even a gift shop on the premises where books, souvenirs, postcards, and an assortment of Civil War paraphernalia were available. That sounded pretty darn commercial to them.

She didn't seem to be holding out for more money, which was also odd. The number of zeroes behind the dollar sign was usually the deciding factor in changing people's minds, Sam had always reasoned with a fair share of cynicism. After Miss Southern's first refusal, his company had counteroffered with more than the standard leasing fee. Darren had also supplied a detailed summary of how Maddox Hill would be used, which wouldn't require any structural changes to either the mansion itself or any of the surrounding land. Wild Oats Productions would provide more than adequate liability insurance to cover the cast, crew, and property. Miss Southern would benefit financially, without losing anything.

The only thing they wanted from her was her signature on the lease form. They would take care of everything else. The answer from her was still the same. No.

At least she had finally agreed to meet with Sam in person, although her lawyer had informed Darren that it was only a courtesy on her part. She wouldn't be changing her mind.

Arriving at the address he'd been given, Sam thought he was at the wrong place until he saw, to the left of an imposing set of double doors, a discreet brass sign with the attorney's name engraved on it. The building looked like someone's elegant home rather than a place of business. Inside, the foyer had a gray marble floor and a ten-foot-high ceiling. Sam raised a brow when he saw an elaborate crystal chandelier hanging from an embellished plasterwork ceiling. And this was only the entryway, he thought.

He walked over to a door on his left, which had another brass nameplate announcing the office of Judson Quill, Attorney-at-Law. The door swung open silently to reveal a tightly permed middle-aged woman seated at a demure mahogany Queen Anne writing desk. A modern computer system was sitting on another table to her right, which was the only indication Sam could see that showed the office was aware of the twentieth century.

The secretary peered at him suspiciously over the top of her half glasses. "May I help you?"

Sam detected an English accent in her clipped tone and a hint of frost in her eyes. She evidently knew the feelings and prejudices of her employer and his client when they pertained to uppity filmmakers, and in this case, she agreed with them.

"Sam Horne," he announced. "I have an appointment with Mr. Quill and Miss Southern."

The woman nodded once, lifted her telephone receiver, and pushed a button on the phone with a forefinger that was tipped with a lethally long polished fingernail. After listening to the party on the other end for a few seconds, she gave Sam's name with all the warmth of an ice-packed refrigerator.

She hung up and indicated a door with a flourish of her manicured hand. As Sam walked to the door the only sound in the room was the hum of the computer. The deep-pile carpet absorbed his steps, making him think of quicksand sucking at his feet. The silence in the office was oppressive and intimidating, making him feel like a little boy again, when his mother used to take him to the public library and told him to sit still and be quiet. Not an easy task for an active, restless kid. Actually, he thought wryly, he'd have trouble doing that as an adult.

Sam opened the door, and his gaze went directly to a large slab of a desk and the unsmiling man in his late fifties seated behind it. Having set up enough photographic shots for maximum effect,

Sam could only admire the arrangement of the two high-back leather chairs, positioned so that the lawyer would be viewed between them when someone entered his office.

Mr. Quill reminded Sam of a character straight out of a Charles Dickens novel. Iron-gray hair, golden-rimmed round glasses perched on a bulbous nose, and a generously rounded paunch suppressed by a tailored brown vest under a brown suit jacket. Mr. Pickwick.

Sam's lawyer in San Francisco usually wore jeans, a blue chambray shirt, occasionally a tie, and a much-worn tan sport coat with suede patches on the elbows. Mr. Quill would undoubtedly have apoplexy if required to meet Carl Trenton across a conference table, Sam thought with amusement.

He hadn't expected the red-carpet treatment, but a little common courtesy would have been nice, he reflected as he crossed the room. Since he didn't see any sign of the Southern woman, he wondered if the lady was even going to show. Hopefully, she was just late. He'd had his fill of delays on this project. At this point, he would agree to just about any concession in order to get the use of her property. Within reason, he mentally tacked on, remembering Darren's latest lecture on the financial costs of this venture.

Stepping between the two chairs, Sam extended his right hand toward the lawyer, who hadn't even had the good manners to stand. He let his hand drop when he caught an intriguing glimpse of a feminine leg crossed over the other at the knee. Something about that leg looked familiar, so he scanned up the leg to the hips, waist, breasts, and finally settled his gaze on the face of the woman who had interfered with his filming earlier.

He stared at her.

She stared back.

"Hello, Red," he finally said with a warmth that he hadn't planned.

"Hello, Wolf," Brett answered.

TWO

As he examined her face Sam realized Brett Southern had known who he was all along. He couldn't detect even a hint of surprise in her stunning green eyes. His gaze narrowed as he remembered the way she'd sauntered across the street in front of his cameras, and he wondered if she'd purposely set out to hinder the progress of his film.

"I didn't disrupt your filming on purpose earlier today," she said. "Although I will understand if you don't believe me."

"Do you read minds too?" he asked.

She shrugged. "I would have thought the same thing if I were in your shoes."

Turning his back to the lawyer, Sam half sat on the edge of the desk. He crossed his arms over his chest and studied the woman who was obviously destined to be a thorn in his side one way or the other. She had discarded the red hooded jacket and replaced the torn panty hose, he noticed as his gaze roamed over her with a thoroughness he usually reserved for his work.

She was definitely not pregnant, he ascertained as he took in her flat stomach under a slim Wedgwood-blue skirt. Her heels and suit jacket matched her skirt, more additions he noticed since their previous meeting. Her shapely legs and teasing smile were the same as before.

She'd disciplined her auburn hair by clasping the lustrous mass at the nape of her slender neck. Her hair should be free to blow in the breeze, he thought. And be stroked by a man's hand.

Her eyes met his easily, no coy glances or blatantly sensual looks.

"Miss Brett Southern, I presume?"

She nodded, lifting her right hand.

He took it within his own, but neither shook it nor released it. "Pregnant, unmarried, and a pain in the butt. You've got a lot going for you, Red."

Mr. Quill made a sound of indignation as he scraped his chair back. "You can't talk to my client in such a rude manner, young man. I won't have it." He came around the desk and stood like an indignant penguin on the other side of Brett's chair. "If you have anything to say to Miss Southern, I suggest you address all your comments to me, Mr. Horne."

Sam's thumb stroked over the back of Brett's smaller hand. Soft, he thought absently. Like warm silk.

Keeping his gaze on her, he said, "I don't think that will be necessary, Mr. Quill. We know each other very well."

Mr. Quill blinked rapidly as he glanced from Sam to Brett, then back again to the man half sitting on his desk. "You know each other? I don't understand. How is that possible?"

"We go way back, don't we, Red?" Sam said.

"Heavens, yes," she drawled. "It must be all of an hour now. In Mr. Horne's business, that probably constitutes a lifetime commitment, Judson."

Sam didn't like her implication, but he let it go, giving her one point for a quick retort. "So you see how ridiculous it would be to chat through a third person when we can just as easily talk to each other."

Straightening to his full height, Mr. Quill wrapped his dignity around himself like a comforting cloak. "If you are so well acquainted with Miss Southern, you would know that she is not in the family way. She also does not like tasteless expressions such as a pain in the . . ."

When the lawyer couldn't bring himself to end Sam's earlier phrase, Brett did so in a dry voice. "I believe Mr. Horne called me a pain in the butt, Judson. To be fair, that's probably an adequate description of how he considers my part in the delay of his documentary. Could I have my hand back, Mr. Horne? Even though I have another one, I've grown rather fond of this one and might need it later."

Sam was amazed at the reluctance he felt when he relaxed his grip on her hand. He'd originally retained his hold only to make a point of being the one in control. He hadn't expected to like the feel of her skin. Or to wonder what the rest of her felt like underneath the clothes she wore.

"If you aren't with child," he said, "why were you carrying all that baby stuff in the basket?"

"It's my business."

"Come on, Red," he said coaxingly. "Don't get all standoffish on me. Not now that we've become so close. It's a perfectly normal question under the circumstances."

She gave him a half smile. "You misunderstood. Gift baskets are my business. I own Southern Touch, a store that designs and sells candies and cakes in specialty baskets for a variety of occasions. I was delivering a friend's order for a baby-shower gift when I accidentally trespassed across the street you were filming."

"Accidentally?" he asked softly.

"At first," she admitted. "Then when I realized who you were and why you were in Fredericksburg, I decided it might be fun to take my time strolling across the street. I admit it was childish, but I thoroughly enjoyed the experience. Except for the tumble."

He'd thought as much, but liked having it confirmed. "What exactly are your objections to the documentary we're making about the battle of Fredericksburg, Red? If we were filming an

X-rated movie or doing a sleazy exposé, I could understand your opposition. Considering the films I make are fairly respectable, I'm puzzled why you want to halt production."

She stood, which, to Sam's delight, brought her closer to him. "I don't have a problem with the subject of your documentary, Mr. Horne. I just don't want Maddox Hill featured in it at this time."

Mr. Quill spoke then, obviously feeling the need to earn his retainer. "Miss Southern is not required to supply a reason for her decision, Mr. Horne. It is her property to do with as she wishes, and she does not want to have strangers invading her family home."

Sam spoke directly to Brett as though the lawyer wasn't even there. "You can't deny that the plantation is part of history. Your father even wrote a book about Maddox Hill's past. People visit the plantation because of its historical significance and the fact that it's been kept basically the way it was since before the Civil War. You allow visitors to take photographs and tramp through the place. The gift shop sells videocassette tours along with postcards and framed prints of the mansion and the grounds. Why forbid my cameras when you permit tourists to use theirs?"

"Visitors snap photos to show their friends and family back home. Then the pictures are stuck into albums and put away. Your film will be shown to millions of television viewers."

"So your complaint is that the film will attract more visitors to the house?"

She shook her head. "The revenue from admission fees helps to pay for the maintenance on the house and property. More attendance would make my accountant happy."

Mr. Quill again contributed his two cents' worth, which, Sam thought, would net him quite a bit more in his fee. "I repeat, Mr. Horne, Miss Southern is not obligated to explain why she is rejecting your offer. She is an extremely private person who does not want her family home invaded by hordes of people who care little for tradition."

Sam turned his head slowly to pin the attorney with a cold stare. "You don't know what the hell you're talking about, Quill, so butt out until you can contribute something helpful."

The attorney made a stuttering sound, obviously angered. "Well, I never!"

"Well, you should," Sam said, before bringing his gaze back to Brett. "Do you agree with him? Is it my style of directing that's the problem?"

"Of course not. Your work is brilliant, and I'll be tuned in to the program like everyone else when it's on."

"If it isn't that, then what is it?"

Brett walked around the chair and placed her hands on the top of its back as she faced him again. "Since neither you nor your partner have accepted my refusal on paper or over the phone, I asked

Judson to arrange this meeting so I could tell you face-to-face that I won't allow Maddox Hill to be part of your documentary. I'm not holding out for more money or trying to be difficult just for the hell of it. I have my reasons, and they are private. Please accept this as my final word on the matter."

Sam watched her as she nodded curtly to her lawyer and walked to the door. She had a way of moving that was so smooth and graceful, she made his mouth water.

For a few seconds he debated going after her, but he decided to bide his time and find out more about the current owner of Maddox Hill Plantation. He suddenly had a craving to know everything the flame-haired woman thought, did, and wanted. And it had absolutely nothing to do with his work.

In Brett's mind, the situation with Wild Oats Productions and Sam Horne was concluded. During the next couple of days, she went ahead with business as usual without thinking about the documentary or its director.

At least that's what she had intended to do. Thoughts of Sam Horne intruded at the oddest, and not always convenient, times.

Stopped on the street by an acquaintance with a new puppy, Brett was chatting away quite normally when she abruptly thought how the little dog's fur was almost a perfect match to the color of Sam

Horne's eyes. As she stopped midsentence and stared at the dog, the puppy's owner gave her a puzzled look and sidled away. Several other times Brett found herself drifting off into some sort of dream state, staring into space while images of Sam Horne danced in her head.

On Wednesday afternoon, two days after she'd seen Sam in Judson's office, Brett gave a slide presentation about cakes and candies to a local woman's group. She was almost through when she felt the strangest tingling down her spine. It was similar to the feeling she'd experienced in the past, when she walked alone down a dark street and heard the sound of footsteps behind her. Considering she was with a group of highly respectable matronly women, sitting in a darkened private room in the city library, she couldn't understand why she was suddenly feeling so apprehensive.

She continued showing the slides featuring chocolate desserts and candy confections made by herself and other experts. Each was more elaborate and exotic than the previous, drawing sounds of delicious agony and wonder from the audience. She announced the creator of each culinary masterpiece and the restaurant where they worked at the time the item had been created. When she came to the Victorian white chocolate baskets she'd made, she included the name of the hotel restaurant in New York where she'd been chocolatier and cake artist until a year earlier.

It wasn't until she asked that the lights be

turned on that she discovered why she'd felt edgy. The reason was standing in the back of the room, leaning against the wall with his arms folded across his chest.

Dressed in a black shirt and tight blue jeans, Sam Horne exuded enough male presence to turn a few heads in his direction, even though he was standing behind the women and had done nothing to draw attention to himself.

When he noticed Brett frowning at him, he smiled and nodded.

Luckily, Brett had given similar lectures in the past and was able to field the questions from the audience with the section of her mind that wasn't wondering why Sam Horne was there.

The women's comments and questions gradually wound down, and they gave Brett a polite ovation for her presentation. When she opened a cardboard box containing heart-shaped boxes made of white chocolate with tiny pink rosebuds and green leaves on each lid, the applause rose considerably. The boxes could be filled with candy or eaten as they were, she told them. The president of the group then announced that Brett had made the confections for everyone to take home with them as examples of the art of candy making.

After the meeting was adjourned, several women came up to Brett to chat about some of the things they'd found fascinating, or to ask questions they had been too timid to raise earlier. Brett smiled and talked to the women, hoping she gave halfway intelligent responses to remarks that held only half her attention. Sam continued to watch her from the back of the room, and she continued to be aware of him every second.

Kathryn Quill, the wife of her attorney, separated from a cluster of four women who had been examining their souvenir candy containers.

"Brett, you are so clever," she said, gushing with a sweetness guaranteed to put even a honeybee in sugar shock. "I would never be able to make such complicated confections in a million, trillion years."

Brett smiled stiffly. Kathryn Quill often specialized in being helpless, although she usually reserved that role for occasions when men were present. The only male in the room was too far away to hear Kathryn's soft, kittenish purr, which always grated on Brett's ears like fingernails on a blackboard.

"I'm sure you would be able to do anything you set your mind to, Kathryn."

The older woman flapped her hands in front of her, waving Brett's compliment away as though it were made of smoke. "You always have something nice to say about everyone. Just like your dear mother. What do you hear from Phillip? Is your father well?"

"Quite well. The rain has slowed down the excavation of the Mayan ruin, but he's keeping busy translating the stone engravings on the steps he uncovered two months ago."

Leaning forward, Kathryn lowered her voice and said in a confidential tone, "I know you miss him. But it's for the best, don't you think? Jud and I feel Phillip is better off keeping busy, so he doesn't have time to dwell on the loss of poor Melanie."

Brett was saved from having to answer by the president of the club raising her voice to dismiss the group and remind them of the next meeting.

Kathryn pressed her powdered cheek against Brett's and kissed the air. "We want you to come for dinner one night soon."

"I'll try," she answered vaguely. "I'll call you."

The lawyer's wife smiled and patted Brett's cheek before fluttering away. Wearing a yellow suit with matching yellow shoes, she made Brett think of a hyper canary.

As the women trickled out of the meeting room, Brett began to gather her things. She was putting the slide carousel in its case when she became aware that Sam was approaching her.

"How kind of you to wait so you can carry my equipment out to my van for me, Mr. Horne."

Amusement glittered in his eyes. "Is that what I'm doing?"

She handed him the rolled-up screen and the slide projector. "It is if you want to talk to me, which is obviously why you're here. Unless you've decided to change careers and take up catering."

"I don't think so."

"Pity," she said as she collected the empty box that had contained the souvenir candy boxes. "Catering would give you something to do between epics."

"There isn't much demand for peanut-butter sandwiches and French toast."

"Is that all you know how to cook?"

"That's about it."

Brett thought the combination was a bit odd, but it was his stomach, not hers.

"If there was something you wanted," she said, "you'll have to tell me on the way out. I have a ton of things to do today, and I don't have the time to stand around and chat about the weather. Or Maddox Hill."

"You found time to chat to those women about chocolate."

Resigned to a delay, Brett took a deep breath and set the rest of the equipment back on the table. "These little lectures help business. I don't do as many as I did when I first took over the shop a year ago, but I still get invitations once in a while to speak to a group, and that never hurts sales. Plus, I get to show off some of the confections and chocolates I made when I worked in New York."

"New York?"

She smiled at the surprised look on his face. "I'm sure you've heard of it, Mr. Horne. It's a big city on the East Coast, has lots of people, the best bagels in the world, and Broadway plays. It's been in all the papers at one time or another."

"I'm familiar with New York, Red," he said dryly. "I hadn't realized you had lived there."

"You weren't listening very closely to my speech, were you? I mentioned the name of the hotel where I worked."

"I was looking at the pictures," he said. "From what I saw a few minutes ago, you were damn good at creating those elaborate chocolate thingies. They looked too pretty to eat."

A compliment of sorts, she supposed. "I still am good at making those thingies, as you so elegantly call them. There's just less of a demand for them here than there was in New York."

"So why did you come back here to settle for something less than what you wanted?"

"I never said I settled for anything," she said with more of a defensive attitude than she wanted to convey.

"You didn't have to say it. I saw your face and heard the pride in your voice when you described your own creations."

"So you were listening, after all."

"I might have caught a word or two. I noticed all of your fancy stuff was when you worked in New York. I don't remember a single one being from your shop here in Fredericksburg."

"Most of the women present have seen the type of things I sell at Southern Touch. I've found that audiences enjoy the more exotic designs, pieces they would never make, nor probably ever see unless they went to a large cosmopolitan city."

"You still haven't said why you left New York."

"Haven't I? It's probably because I don't think

it's any of your business." Brett picked up the bag of equipment again after draping the strap of her purse over her shoulder. "Either carry those things to my van or give them to me, Mr. Horne. The library has another meeting scheduled for this room and I have a busy schedule."

She stepped around him and walked toward the door. Sam followed, carrying the things she'd handed to him. He didn't ask any more questions until they reached her store's van in the parking lot. A logo on the side announced the shop's name and displayed a paintbrush stroking a dab of color on a lollipop in the shape of a rose.

After she unlocked the van, Brett slid open the side panel and set the bag inside. Sam didn't wait for her to take the rest of the equipment from him. He came alongside her and placed the screen and projector on the floor of the van. There was plenty of room for her belongings, but not all that much space for the two of them in the opening of the van.

Brett turned to move out of the way at the same time Sam straightened beside her. For a few tense moments their eyes met and held, their expressions serious and intense. And puzzled.

Sam lifted his hand to touch her face, running a knuckle gently over her cheek. "I wondered," he said aloud, although Brett had the impression he was talking more to himself than to her.

"Wondered what?"

"How your skin would feel."

"Is this a type of scientific survey you do often?"

He smiled and shook his head. "This is a first. I can't remember when I was this curious about a woman. You intrigue me, Red. I'm not altogether sure I like it."

"Then perhaps you should find something you like to do and leave me alone." She tilted her head to one side and studied him. "Which part do you find curious, Mr. Horne? The bit about me turning down all that lovely money your production company has offered? Or why I wouldn't want hordes of people trampling all over my mother's plantation? Or is it just that you like to get your own way?"

Instead of becoming irritated by her barely disguised sarcasm, he said, "All of the above and then some." The amused tone of his voice changed. "I'd like to talk to you."

She sighed wearily. "I'm not going to change my mind, Mr. Horne. I'm sorry you and your staff are being inconvenienced, but you shouldn't have taken it for granted I was going to buckle under and let you on the property."

Relentless as a mosquito, Sam attacked the problem. "Since you're familiar with the area, I was hoping you could suggest an alternative solution to our little problem."

"*Our* little problem, Mr. Horne?"

"Call me Sam. The way you say my last name

makes me think you're picturing me with horns and a pitchfork."

Brett glanced at her watch. "I've promised to stop by and see someone this afternoon. I can't disappoint her. Then I have a lot of work to do at the shop. I don't have much spare time today."

"Would I be in the way if I came with you?"

"Probably. Why would you want to waste your time riding around with me when you have a film to make?"

"It's my time. And I wouldn't call being with you a waste of it."

Brett thought about his request for a minute, then surprised them both by agreeing to take him with her. "I usually stay a couple of hours where I'm going. The woman I'm going to see has ancestors who lived in this area during the War Between the States. You can put the visit down as research if it will ease your conscience for taking time away from your film."

"You certainly worry about my conscience a great deal," he said casually. "That's the second time you've mentioned it."

Brett opened the driver's door of the van. "Someone has to. It doesn't seem to bother you all that much."

It wasn't until he had settled in the passenger seat that he replied to her comment. "Why should my conscience bother me? I'm making a movie, not robbing a bank."

She backed out of the parking spot and didn't answer until she had stopped at a red light.

"I'm sorry," she said quietly.

He turned his head to look at her. "For what?"

"You only want to do your job, and I've been giving you a hard time over something that isn't your fault."

Sam had always considered himself intelligent, able to comprehend most situations without too much trouble. He certainly was having trouble understanding Brett Southern, though. And he wanted to, he realized. Very much.

He didn't have a clue what she was thinking or feeling. What baffled him even more was that he couldn't figure out *why* it was important for him to know what made her tick. It was, though. So far she'd allowed only glimpses of the woman underneath, and Sam was determined to discover all of her.

At least he understood the physical attraction drawing him toward her. He understood that it was more potent than anything he'd felt for any other woman. Every time he was with Brett, he plumbed new depths of the desire growing steadily between them.

One way to find answers was to ask questions. "What isn't my fault?" he asked.

She shook her head. "It doesn't matter."

He wanted to pursue her puzzling remark, but he didn't feel this was the time to push. As she left the city limits he asked, "Where are we going?"

"I'm going to visit my mother's closest friend, Abigail Nelson. Abbie lost her sight a little over a year ago from a flash fire on her stove. I try to see her at least once a week." She smiled. "Abbie taught me how to make my first batch of candy when I was about eight or nine. Her bakery in Old Town used to turn out the most fabulous cakes decorated with delicate flowers made from spun sugar and royal icing that were in great demand for weddings and showers. When I moved back to Fredericksburg, I took over the bakery she could no longer run after her accident. The arrangement benefited both of us. She still has an income and I didn't have to make many changes in order to convert to making candy."

"So she's your silent partner?"

"Once you meet her, you'll realize the word silent rarely applies to Abbie, but that's as good a term as any. Over the years she's taught me various tricks of the trade, which put me at the top of my class at culinary school. I've learned a great deal from her. It's a debt I'll never be able to repay."

"I wondered how you got into the confectionary business." He chuckled. "And I'm also curious how you stay so slim. Don't you eat what you make?"

"I have a friend in New York who's a sculptor. She uses clay and hasn't once been tempted to eat any of her work. I just use chocolate and royal icing instead of clay."

"So you consider yourself a pastry artist?"

"The title doesn't matter, the result does." Smiling, she added, "One of my instructors threw us bits of advice along with instructions on how to cool a copper bowl before whipping cream. His favorite was a Zen saying about the journey being more important than the destination."

"The work is what's significant, not the product at the end," Sam said. "That's how it is with a film. I'm involved, challenged, and energized by the subject while I'm filming. Once it's finished, I always have a letdown feeling, almost an emptiness deep inside that isn't filled until I start another project."

Brett was stunned by the insight into his emotions. She wanted to believe his revelation had been prompted by an honest desire to share a part of himself with her, rather than be suspicious about his motive in showing her his "sensitive side." She was going to have to reevaluate what she thought about Sam Horne, the director and the man.

She turned off the main road onto a narrower street, taking the curves at a reasonable speed, easing around an indention in the road with practiced skill. Houses became fewer on either side of the road, then stopped altogether when she drove onto a gravel lane only wide enough for the van.

If Sam didn't know better, he would have said the house at the end of the lane was where Little Red Riding Hood's grandmother lived. White gingerbread trim followed the lines of the eaves on the sprawling white one-story home, and along the roof and the railing on the porch. Plants grew in long narrow window boxes under each window, some of them still boasting blossoms of assorted colors. The three rocking chairs on the porch were painted different colors: one a bright red, another a brilliant blue, and the last an emerald green.

Brett parked in front of the house and smiled when she saw him staring. "Abbie liked bright colors when she had her sight. Abbie's daughter and I just repainted everything the way it was when Abbie lost her sight so she can still visualize what is actually there."

She tapped the horn twice, then paused and honked one more time. As she got out of the van the front door opened and Sam saw a woman about Brett's age come out onto the porch. She was strikingly beautiful, dressed in a light gray suit with a cameo pin at the collar of her immaculate cream silk blouse. Her skin was a warm coffee tone, and her jet-black hair was combed back and secured at her nape with a gray scarf.

"I hope you brought Momma some candy, Brett," she called out. "She just finished that box of amaretto bonbons."

Brett opened the side panel of the van and took out a large box similar to the one she'd taken to the library. Carrying it with both hands, she walked toward the porch where Elsa waited. Sam was right behind her, well aware that her friend was watching him with avid curiosity.

At the bottom of the steps, Brett introduced

them. "Elsa, I'm sure you've heard about the documentary that's being made about the battle of Fredericksburg. This is Sam Horne. He's the director of the film. Sam, this is Elsa Nelson. She's a pediatrician, and my best friend."

Sam extended his right hand, stepping up onto the porch to greet Elsa. "It's a pleasure to meet one of Red's friends."

Elsa glanced at Brett. "Red?"

"He first saw me when I was wearing my red coat, so he thinks the nickname is cute."

"And he's still alive?"

"I've tagged him 'the Big Bad Wolf,' and since it's be-kind-to-animals week . . ." Brett shrugged.

Sam scowled. "If you two are quite through, I'd like to add that I'm relieved to see Red has such a charming friend. So far she's only introduced me to Judson Quill."

Elsa chuckled at the lack of enthusiasm in his voice. "Judson is an acquired taste. You have the town buzzing with excitement, Mr. Horne. Is it true you're going to use some of the local people in the documentary?"

He nodded. "Mostly people who belong to re-enactment groups and their families. My producer practically danced on the ceiling when he heard they all have their own uniforms and firearms. He's able to save a small fortune by not having to supply their costumes and equipment. The main characters have all been cast, but we'll use local people for extras."

"What about slaves?" Elsa asked with cool steadiness. "Are you depicting any examples of slavery in your film?"

"I don't like the concept of slavery any better than you do, Dr. Nelson, but it was a part of that time period. It would be dishonest to pretend it didn't exist and an insult to the people who endured slavery with dignity and courage."

Elsa gave him a long, careful look before she turned to Brett. "He's smart, sensitive, and attractive. You don't find that combination very often, Brett. You'd better grab this one before someone else does."

Brett gave her friend a glowering glance. "Don't you have any babies waiting for you in your office?"

Elsa checked her watch. "Actually, I do. I just stopped in to check on Momma. She had a headache when I left this morning."

Suddenly serious, Brett asked, "Is she all right? She's been getting those headaches fairly frequently."

Elsa's dark eyes were troubled. "She won't agree to go to the doctor to be examined. You know how she is. She says she's been poked and stabbed enough with needles to last two lifetimes."

Brett put her hand on Elsa's arm. "We'll gang up on her. If that doesn't work, we'll figure something else out."

Elsa hugged Brett, then said to Sam, "I was going to warn you that my mother can be remarkably blunt when she wants to be, but I think you can handle yourself no matter what the situation."

"Elsa Ann." The firm voice came from behind them. Sam turned to see a shadowy figure standing behind the screen door, a woman of small stature with a commanding voice. "You have been taught better manners than to leave guests on the front porch. Invite Brett's young man inside."

"Yes, Momma," Elsa said obediently as though she were six and not twenty-nine. "Please go inside, Mr. Horne, or Momma will be very unhappy with me." Elsa winked at Brett, then added, "I'm going back to the clinic now, Momma. If you need anything, you call me. Promise?"

"Yes, yes. Go on with you, child. You needn't fret about me. I'll have a grand time entertaining Brett's gentleman friend."

"All right, Momma." Elsa raised an eyebrow at Brett, silently asking if Brett knew what she was doing.

Brett smiled and shrugged.

"I heard that," Abbie said.

Elsa and Brett stared at each other, then laughed.

"How does she do that?" Elsa asked. "You be good, Momma, you hear me?"

"Of course I heard you, Elsa Ann. I'm blind, not deaf. Now off with you. It isn't every day I have an attractive man come calling, and I want to enjoy every minute."

Brett saw Sam was grinning broadly. She shifted her attention to Elsa. "I'll call you later."

"You'd better," her friend murmured with a crooked grin and a quick glance at Sam.

Elsa lifted a hand in farewell to Sam and hurried down the steps. "It's a pleasure to meet you, Mr. Horne," she called over her shoulder. "I have a feeling I'll be seeing you again."

As Elsa climbed into her car the screen door opened, its hinges complaining slightly. Abbie Nelson stepped out onto the porch, keeping her hand on the door. She was a woman of medium height, but appeared frail due to her thin frame and delicate features. Dark glasses shielded her scarred sightless eyes, the only indication of her disability. Sam was amused to see she was wearing a baseball player's shirt with the Chicago Cubs insignia on the front and black stirrup pants.

Abbie turned her head unerringly in Brett's direction. "Is that rum-flavored chocolates I smell?"

"And some truffles I know you like." Brett kissed Abbie's cheek before introducing Sam. "Sam Horne is directing a documentary about the battle of Fredericksburg, Abbie. Sam, I'd like you to meet Abigail Nelson."

Sam stepped closer and took the older woman's hand. "I understand you've known Brett since she was born. Maybe you're just the person I need to talk to."

Abbie tilted her head back as if she were looking right at him. "That depends on what you want to know."

"For starters, what makes her tick."

"Men don't need to know how a woman thinks. It only confuses the issue."

Sam grinned. "Men are confused enough trying to figure out the female mind. We need every advantage we can get."

"From the sound of you and the fact Brett brought you here, you don't have too much to worry about. Now tell me, Mr. Horne, do you like baseball?"

"Yes, ma'am." Sam glanced again at the Cubs insignia on her shirt and said somberly, "I'm partial to the San Francisco Giants myself."

The older woman scoffed at his choice. As she began rattling off an impressive list of statistics about the Cubs—the team he should be following —she took his arm and drew him with her into the house. She broke off her discourse to ask over her shoulder, "Are you coming, Brett?"

Amused, Brett followed behind them. "I'm here, Abbie. Why don't you take Sam into the trophy room while I make iced tea for all of us?"

Abbie liked that idea and added one of her own. "Mr. Horne can take the chocolates so your hands will be free."

Brett smiled widely as she handed over the box to Sam. His gaze went to her lips, then slowly raised to meet her eyes. His own mouth curved into a sensual smile, and for a moment Brett couldn't move, could hardly breathe.

Abbie broke the spell with her usual frankness. "You two can ogle each other later. Right now I want to show my boys' trophies to Mr. Horne."

Sam blinked and stared at Brett. Echoing Elsa's earlier statement, he murmured, "How does she do that?"

Laughing, Brett left them and walked into the kitchen. She took her time making the iced tea. Abbie had little variety in the people who came to see her, and Sam would be good company for her. How Brett knew that about him mystified her, since she had known him for only a matter of hours. But there was something about him that implied strength and intelligence laced with a liberal dash of humor. His self-confidence could be irritating if it wasn't so natural, as much a part of his makeup as the color of his eyes and hair.

She heard Abbie laughing as she carried the tray of drinks into the room where the older woman kept the awards earned by the Little League baseball teams she sponsored every year. Sam was seated on the old leather couch beside Abbie, who was showing him a scrapbook of pictures Elsa had collected over the years. The two of them, Brett noticed, were already on a first-name basis. As they paged through the scrapbook Sam would read a caption under a picture, and Abbie would tell an anecdote about the occasion, the person, or the game played that day.

During the rest of the visit, Brett was sent out of the room on one pretext after the other by Abbie. She raised a window, watered the houseplants that didn't need any water, and freshened the pitcher of tea twice. Brett didn't really mind. Abbie was having a great time with her male guest, who made her laugh and who listened enthusiastically to all her stories, stories that Brett and Elsa had heard many times before.

When Brett returned to the trophy room after retrieving Abbie's shawl from her bedroom, the older woman stopped talking as she heard Brett enter the room.

Suspicious of the sudden silence, Brett said, "I hope you aren't boring Sam with all those naughty episodes you remember of my misspent youth, Abbie. He can come up with enough stuff to pester me about without your help."

Abbie immediately started to tell some humorous stories involving Brett and Elsa. Brett alternated between amusement and embarrassment depending on the anecdote.

Sam laughed at all the stories, but he was particularly intrigued by the one about how Brett and Elsa had built a tree house in an old apple tree at Maddox Hill. Instead of good solid wood, the girls had used cardboard boxes they'd hoisted up to a suitable spot, then tied together and secured to the tree limbs.

"They spent hours and hours in their multiroom tree house," Abbie said, "until the first thunderstorm came along. The rain soaked the cardboard and they were left with a soggy mess."

Brett added, "You might mention that we were eight years old at the time. We had made dollhouses out of cardboard boxes, so we thought we could do the same for a tree house."

"Perfectly understandable," Sam said. "Wonderful things, cardboard boxes. I once made a herd of cattle out of big boxes I got from a grocery store."

Both women said at the same time, "A herd of cattle?"

He nodded. "I had collected sixteen boxes and I lined them up in a corral made from a rope wound around some trees in our backyard. I stuck a tree branch at one end of each box for horns and a section of frayed rope at the other for tails. I roped them, branded them, and drove them across mountain ranges and raging rivers. I even rode one or two until they collapsed."

"How old were you?" Abbie asked.

He shrugged, then remembered Abbie couldn't see the gesture. "I don't know for sure. Nine or ten."

"An imagination can create such wonderful worlds," Abbie said. "Were you raised on a ranch?"

"Only in my mind. I grew up in San Francisco. The neighborhood didn't have many children my age except girls, so I made up things to do by myself." He grinned. "It wasn't until I was older that I appreciated girls."

Abbie laughed. "Now that I believe. That reminds me of the time when Brett wanted to invite a certain young man to her seventh birthday party. She was totally smitten until Billy Sheldon tried to kiss her as she opened her presents. She decked him."

Sam roared with laughter.

Brett groaned.

Before Abbie could catch her second wind and regale Sam with more of her adventures, Brett said, "We need to get going, Abbie. I have a lot to do and I'm sure Sam does too."

"I understand," Abbie said. "I've enjoyed meeting you, Sam. I hope you'll find time to visit again. I'd like to hear more about your work."

Standing beside her, Sam bent down and kissed her cheek. "And I'd like to hear more about Brett."

Abbie smiled. "I thought you might. Please come anytime. You are always welcome."

"Thank you," he said sincerely.

Brett hugged and kissed Abbie good-bye, then led the way back outside to her van. Sam made a few comments about Abbie as they drove back toward town, then he fell silent. That was fine with Brett. She wasn't feeling particularly chatty either, especially if Sam decided to bring up the subject of Maddox Hill.

He seemed to rouse himself when she asked which hotel he was staying in. After giving her the name, he said, "We haven't talked about Maddox Hill."

"Hmm," she murmured. "And we also haven't disagreed about anything. Why don't we leave it that way?"

"Brett, I'm not asking to use Maddox Hill just for myself, for the convenience of headquartering my crew there. A lot of people are depending on me to make the best documentary I possibly can. I won't even go into the amount of money that's been put up by investors to finance the film. What I'm saying is that I'm not the only one involved. If we have to find another location for the encampment and the hospital scenes, that will run into a lot of wasted money paying a crew that isn't able to do their jobs, not to mention the time spent waiting around for Darren to come up with an alternative location."

She stopped the van at the front entrance of his hotel, then turned to face him. "I'm sorry, Sam. If things were different, perhaps something could be worked out, but this isn't the time."

"Would there ever be a good time?"

"I don't know." She looked away. "I wish I did."

Before he could pursue the matter further, his door was opened by the hotel doorman.

"Will you be at Maddox later tonight?" he asked her.

"Probably not. I have some work to do at the shop." She hesitated, then asked, "What if you could use the grounds but not the house? Would that help?"

He frowned as he considered it. "I would be able to film the encampment scenes."

"I'll think about it, then."

Brett watched as he unfastened his seat belt and levered his long length out of the van. His "I'll see you later" wasn't a casual remark thrown out in parting.

Brett had no doubts at all that she would indeed be seeing Sam Horne again.

THREE

Brett hummed along with the music coming from the cassette player. Humming she could do. Singing she couldn't. Luckily, the melodious piano music was without any lyrics she would be tempted to mangle.

She couldn't even stand hearing her own voice in the shower. It was just one of life's little jests, she'd decided a long time ago. For as long as she could remember, she'd loved music, any and every kind. But when she was six, her piano teacher had given Brett's mother a refund. Brett could appreciate music all she wanted; she just couldn't make any. Some people were musically inclined. She was musically "disinclined" and half a note away from the one she aimed for most of the time.

The ache in her left shoulder started moving up the scale from uncomfortable to downright painful, so she rotated her arm and flexed her wrist a few times to work some of the tautness out of her muscles. Glancing down at the orders yet to be completed, she grimaced. The stack of unfinished orders was still bigger than the stack of finished ones. She had at least four more hours of work to do before she could quit.

She picked up the decorating bag she'd been using and aimed the fine tip at the candy mold in front of her. Squeezing gently, she filled the top part of each pumpkin impression with a rich green candy mixture that would look like the stem and leaves of the pumpkin after she added the brown chocolate eyes and orange body. She only had to make seventy-five jack-o'-lantern lollipops, which was considerably fewer than the over five hundred she'd had to make for Halloween orders.

After years of experience, she could make the molded candy automatically without having to think about what she was doing. While that made it easier to do the work, she was left with too much time to think.

Usually that wasn't a problem, but that was before Wild Oats Productions had stirred up a hornet's nest by wanting to use Maddox Hill. She couldn't have them or anyone else buzzing around the house and outbuildings until she finished her search.

Her father had finally found some peace after the tragedy involving Brett's mother, and Brett had found a clue to discovering what had really happened to Melanie Southern. Now there was a threat by the name of Sam Horne that could upset her plans.

Perhaps if the documentary were being made by someone not as well-known, she might have gone along with the arrangements. But everywhere Sam Horne went, publicity followed close behind.

Even before he'd won the Emmy, Sam had caught the attention and admiration of the press, first in his hometown of San Francisco, then in Los Angeles, where he'd gotten the technical experience to go along with the ideas he wished to put on film. He was physically attractive, wealthy, talented, successful, and didn't give a damn about his image. The media loved him. The more they wrote about him and talked about him, the less he made himself available for interviews. That only further whetted the ravenous appetite of the public. He hadn't been busted for drugs, driving under the influence, or caught with another man's wife. No one came forward to claim they had his footprints on their backs after he'd walked over them to get to the top. That didn't stop the reporters from focusing on him, especially when he dated a well-known woman. As Brett recalled, there were quite a few of those.

With Sam acting like a beacon for reporters, she couldn't take the chance of having her mother's alleged suicide resurrected by the media and reporters snooping around for a new slant to an old story.

The presence of Sam and his crew at Maddox

Hill would also interfere with her private investigation. According to the information she'd received from the producer, several rooms were to be converted into a hospital for wounded Confederates and a few of the outbuildings used for horses and equipment. More than that, Sam wanted some of the crew to stay in the house and the rest on the grounds, along with the reenactors' large encampment.

Her systematic search of the house would be nearly impossible with Sam and his group underfoot, and she'd already waited long enough to find the answers behind her mother's mysterious death.

As she continued filling molds Brett at first attributed the repetitive pounding sound she heard to the taped music. After a minute she realized someone was knocking on the door of the shop. Evidently the person couldn't read, she thought with irritation. She distinctly remembered turning the sign on the door to the side that stated the shop was closed.

After wiping her hands on a damp towel, she snapped on the lights in the shop and walked out of the back room. Mumbling several choice words of an unfriendly nature under her breath, she walked around the counter and several display tables to reach the door.

She stopped and stared.

Through the gap in the tied-back lace curtains on the glass panel of the door, she saw a man's black shirt tucked into jeans fastened by a black leather belt. Sam Horne. If asked, she wouldn't have been able to say how she could recognize the man only by a small portion of his anatomy, but she knew.

Like she knew taxes were due on the fifteenth of April. Like she knew the roof in her bedroom would leak when it rained. Like she knew the most momentous moments of her life—good and bad—happened when she least expected them.

He had to have seen the lights go on in the shop, she thought as he knocked again, obviously impatient. Apparently he was accustomed to people moving faster in response to his demands.

Approaching the door, she pointed to the closed sign. His response was to apply his knuckles once more to the door. She stabbed at the sign again. He knocked again.

Refusing to shout at him through the glass pane, she unlocked the dead bolt and opened the door. The bell over her head clanged several times. "The store is closed," she said.

"That's okay. I don't plan on buying anything."

She pursed her lips and murmured, "Ah."

"What does that mean?"

"I see. I understand," she explained, as though talking to a rather dim bulb. "It could also be a substitute for then-what-the-hell-do-you-want?"

He grinned. "That's a lot for such a small word."

"I know another short word that conveys a succinct message."

His eyes glittered with humor. "And you're dying to tell me what it is."

She smiled sweetly. "It's good-bye. Isn't that a good word?"

He nodded. "Used in the proper context, it's a terrific word, but it doesn't apply in this situation. An invitation to come in would work wonders, though."

Brett started to argue the point, but a bell dinged in the back room at that moment. If she continued her debate with Sam, she would ruin a batch of candy by letting it stay in the refrigerator too long.

She stepped to one side and gestured for him to come in. "Shut the door and lock it again, please. There's some scarecrows that need my attention in the back room or I would do it myself. I don't want any more late-night visitors."

She didn't wait around to see if he did as she asked. Removing the scarecrow lollipops from the refrigerator took priority over entertaining Mr. Sam Horne. She took the mold, with its scarecrows made of four different colors of chocolate candy, and turned it upside down to release the scarecrows onto a clean cloth spread out on a long worktable. Next to them were lollipops in the shapes of autumn leaves and ears of multicolored Indian corn.

Brett worked quickly and efficiently, wiping down the mold and starting to fill it again by applying the first color, which was yellow for the hands, eyes, nose, and hair. When she was through, she slid the tray back into the refrigerator and set the timer again.

She didn't need to look up to know Sam had finally followed her into the workroom. At the moment she didn't want to analyze why she was so aware of every move he made.

Or why her palms became damp and her mouth went dry every time she looked at him.

"You have an interesting selection of merchandise out front," he said as he leaned his hip against the table she was using. "I didn't realize suckers came in that many varieties."

She quirked a brow. "Suckers come in all sizes and shapes. Wasn't it P. T. Barnum who said there was a sucker born every minute? I try very hard not to be one myself."

He gestured toward the lollipops spread out on the table. "I was talking about those things with the sticks in them."

"Oh, those suckers," she said with a cocky grin. "One of the women who works for me is from England and she refers to them as lollies. Whatever you want to call them, they are the backbone of the store."

He picked up one of the completed pumpkin lollipops and bit into it. Brett silently told herself she now needed to make seventy-six more, not seventy-five.

Sam gave her an odd look. "This tastes like pumpkin pie."

"Good. It's supposed to." She looked up as he

was reaching for another one. "I'm glad you like the merchandise, Mr. Horne, but the more you eat, the more I have to make to fill orders."

He took one anyway. "So that's why you're here instead of at home."

"How did you know I wasn't home?"

"I phoned the private number at the plantation. There was no answer."

"For good reason. I don't stay there when I work late in the shop."

He had started to reach for another piece of candy, but stopped to look at her. "You don't live at the plantation? Where do you live, then?"

She didn't correct his idea that she didn't live at Maddox Hill. She pointed upward. "I fixed the rooms above this shop into an apartment." She bent over another mold. "What brings you here at this hour of the night, Mr. Horne? Or should I guess?"

"You still haven't told me why you don't want us to film on your property."

She continued working, her movements automatic. "I believe I did say I have my reasons."

"Yes, you did. But you didn't say what they were. I thought we might discuss your reservations and come to some kind of agreement."

"I thought we already had. You just won't accept it."

Sam was watching her hands as she expertly filled the pumpkin molds with orange-colored chocolate. "Can I try that?"

Surprised by his request, she looked up. "Why?"

His lopsided smile did odd things to her insides. "You have a very suspicious nature, Red. You should work on that. I, on the other hand, have a curious nature. I like to know how things work." He inclined his head toward her. "And how some people's minds work."

Brett debated for four seconds. Then she stepped back and handed the decorator bag to him. "Here you go."

He stared at the cone-shaped cloth as though it would detonate. "What do I do with this?"

She smiled slowly, her eyes shining with mischief. Laughter was in her voice when she replied, "You don't really want me to answer that, do you?"

Sam felt the tension of arousal coil in his groin when she smiled at him with a provocative gleam in her eyes. She was a sassy handful, and he intended to put his hands on her real soon.

"Let me put this another way," he drawled. "Would you please show me how to work this whatever-it-is?"

She twisted the top to push the tinted chocolate down toward the tip. Putting the bag in his hand, she wrapped his fingers around it. "When you have the tip over the mold, you squeeze a little to make the melted candy come out. You don't need much pressure, otherwise you'll overflow the mold. Put in only as much as the indentation will hold. Here, let me give you a sheet to practice on. I need these scarecrows for an order."

Sam took the sheet of molds she'd chosen from a slotted shelf above the table and looked at the shapes. "These are pigs!" he said.

"Hmm," she murmured. "So they are."

"I think you've got the wrong fairy tale. As the Big Bad Wolf, I'm supposed to sneak into your grandmother's house, not mess around with the Three Little Pigs' houses."

"That's my great-great-great-grandmother's house," she said, "and I think you'll have more luck huffing and puffing at brick houses than trying to sneak into mine."

He gave her a slow smile that made her insides feel as gooey as the candy in the decorator bag. "We'll see," he said, and turned his attention to the molds.

His first attempt overflowed. Brett didn't remind him to apply pressure to the bag gently. He would figure that out himself. His second one was better, but still too much candy came out. He scraped off the excess with his finger, breaking a number of health codes. Since she didn't plan to sell what he was making, she didn't say anything.

She noticed he didn't let his mistakes remain. They were wiped out and done over until they were correct. She had the proof of something she had suspected. Sam Horne was a perfectionist. That trait was a good one for a film director, but a difficult one for the people around him if he expected them to live up to his standards on a daily basis. She much preferred the other aspect of Sam's nature that she'd recognized easily, his curiosity and avid search for answers. In that, he was just like her father.

Phillip Southern was a well-known archaeologist who had spent his life searching for answers to mysteries that might never be solved. With painstaking detail, he followed each clue, never giving up until he was satisfied he'd explored as much as possible. At the present time he was investigating a recently discovered Mayan village.

The only mystery Dr. Southern hadn't been able to solve, Brett thought ruefully, was why his wife had taken her own life.

She wondered if perhaps she had more of her father's questing nature than she'd originally thought. She knew she wouldn't be able to put an end to the questions that arose from her mother's death until she found the answers.

She continued with her orders, putting another mold in the refrigerator and taking several out. After turning the candy out of the molds, she glanced at Sam. She bit her lip to keep from laughing. He was bent over the pig mold, the tip of his tongue sticking out of the corner of his mouth as he concentrated on filling another one.

She couldn't help wondering if he applied the same intensity to everything he did. That thought provoked some interesting scenarios that she tried to blot out of her mind. If she thought about Sam

Horne, she would have to admit that he wasn't the arrogant, self-absorbed prima donna she'd expected. That man would have been easy to ignore. And to forget. This man wasn't. Brett would find it easier to shrug off an audit by the IRS than to pretend the attraction sizzling around them didn't exist. Or that she wasn't drawn to his sense of humor, his inborn confidence, and the sensitivity she'd witnessed in his films.

She was doing the right thing in not thinking about him.

After consulting her next order, Brett chose the correct mold and continued the procedure, this time making more autumn leaves.

Sam finished his tray and placed his hand on the small of his back as he straightened. "This is more difficult than it looks. What do I do with this?"

"The mold goes on one of the shelves in the fridge for a few minutes to harden."

When Sam opened the door, he stared at the interior. The refrigerator had been specially fitted with a number of shelves approximately three inches apart with several deeper shelves near the top. Most of the racks were empty except for several trays of grinning pumpkins, scarecrows, and preening turkeys. He slid the mold he'd just completed onto one of the shelves, surprised at the sense of satisfaction he felt from doing such a simple thing.

Remembering all the candy bouquets and gift

baskets he'd seen in the other room, he asked, "Do you make all the stuff you pack in the baskets?"

"Just the candy and occasionally some royal icing decorations for a cake. I have two people who help me when there are a lot of orders."

He walked back to the table. "Where are they tonight?"

"I don't need their help tonight."

He picked up the stack of orders and did a fast calculation of the numbers listed on them. "Do you plan on making all these tonight?"

"Hmm," she answered as she continued squeezing the candy into the leaf molds. When he didn't say anything else, she glanced up at him and saw he was frowning. "What?"

"I was going to suggest we go out for a drink somewhere and talk."

Brett turned back to her work. "There's nothing to talk about. I'm not going to change my mind. Besides, I don't drink."

"Not even water?"

"I meant alcohol, and so did you."

"Yeah, I did," he admitted with a wry smile. "I was thinking of the place just down the block, the Twelve Oaks restaurant. Taking a person out for drinks or dinner is the usual procedure when trying to soften him or her up during business negotiations. Though I usually let Darren do all that schmoozing stuff."

"But you were going to make an exception for me? How sweet," she said with a twist of sarcasm.

Her shoulder was sending slashes of pain up to her neck again, so she stopped what she was doing, straightening and shrugging her shoulders.

"What's wrong?" he asked when she grimaced.

"Occupational hazard." She massaged her left shoulder. "I thought I was in pretty good physical shape until I started this business. I made more individual confections at the hotel, but not that many repetitive projects as I do here. The repeated motion and bending over causes some discomfort after a while."

"I noticed. My back was complaining just from doing one of those sheets, and you've done seven in the same amount of time. By the looks of the supply already finished, you were at it for some time before I arrived." He moved away from the table, walking behind her. "Don't tense up any more than you already are," he said as she stiffened the moment he touched her. "Your shoulders are practically up to your ears."

Lord, his hands felt wonderful, she thought as she closed her eyes. "You have such a way with words, Mr. Horne." She made a soft sighing sound. "Your hands aren't bad either."

Sam had to struggle to keep those hands from wandering any farther than her shoulders. Not every woman looked as good from the back as she did from the front, but Brett Southern was the exception. His thumbs brushed over her spine several times, then her slender neck, drawing murmurs of pleasure from her that were not helping him control the massage or his thoughts. What he'd meant as an impersonal gesture to ease the tension in her shoulders was causing him a great deal of discomfort in his own body.

As her taut muscles loosened Brett noticed the difference in the way Sam touched her from when he'd started the massage. His fingers still flexed and rubbed over the cords in her neck and shoulders, but more slowly, and his stroking was definitely more arousing than relaxing. She could have sworn he was standing closer, too, the heat from his body warming her entire back.

The temptation to lean against him was almost stronger than she could resist. Certain parts of her body that he wasn't touching were aching to feel his hands.

She was getting slightly hysterical with panic when the timer went off. Saved by the bell, she thought wildly as she stepped away from him. "Thanks," she said offhandedly, and walked over to the refrigerator.

The cool air flowed over her skin, never so welcome as it was at that moment. She would like to have stood in front of the opened refrigerator longer, but Sam might wonder what she was doing. Or worse, ask her why she was standing there. In the short time she'd known him, he hadn't been shy about asking whatever he wanted to know.

She certainly didn't have an answer for him. Or herself. Her skin felt on fire, and her blood seemed to have turned into molten lava. She didn't understand why she was reacting this way. It wasn't as though she'd never been touched by a man before.

But not this man.

She had to think about which tray she was supposed to take out, which irritated her even more than her response to Sam's touch. Damn him, she thought. He made her forget what she was doing. Finally figuring out the problem, she removed the correct tray and carried it over to a different area of the long table. Turning the mold over, she tapped it to release the candy onto another clean white cloth.

When she felt more in control of herself, she turned around to face him. "I have about three more hours of work. If you want to help, that's fine with me, but I don't think this is how you usually spend your free time. Why don't I just tell you again that I won't allow my mother's home to be invaded by Hollywood, and then you can trot back to your hotel room and sulk."

"San Francisco," he said easily.

"What about it?"

"That's where our headquarters are, not Hollywood."

She shook her head in exasperation. "Are all directors such sticklers for accuracy?"

He shrugged. "Beats me. I haven't worked with that many. Some of my friends are in the same line of work, but we usually don't talk shop when we get together." He inclined his head to one side and watched her with a predatory expression, like a hawk spotting a young chick. "You just referred to the plantation as your mother's. You did that on another occasion. The title is in your name. My producer checked."

Brett stepped over to the sink and turned on the faucet to wash her hands. "Legally, Maddox Hill belongs to me. My mother left it to me in her will."

Sam's eyes narrowed as he watched her. In only a few seconds she'd managed to undo all the good effects of his massage. Perhaps he was to blame by asking her questions about Maddox Hill, which she obviously didn't want to talk about. If she stood any more stiffly, she would snap in two.

His gut instinct was telling him he'd struck a nerve by talking about her mother. A very raw one. Why? he wondered. Perhaps if he prodded a little, he'd uncover a couple of Brett's mysteries. He didn't even try to tell himself it was because he was looking for a way to convince her to let him use her plantation. His interest in this intriguing and enigmatic woman was fast becoming entirely personal.

"The plantation was left to you and not your father?" he asked. "Isn't that a little unusual when the spouse is still alive?"

She grabbed a towel to dry her hands, not looking at him. "My mother was a Maddox, and therefore, so is her daughter. The plantation was originally built as a wedding present for Maletha Maddox, my great-great-great-grandmother, in the early 1800s. She left it to her granddaughter, who married a third cousin named Maddox. My mother's mother also married a distant relative named Maddox." Glancing at him, Brett smiled at his raised eyebrow. "I have a very narrow family tree. The gist of this long-winded explanation is that the property is handed down to the women in the family."

"Are you planning on following the Maddox tradition?"

"Alas, the supply of Maddox cousins has dwindled over the years."

"Do you have any man hovering around you on a regular basis?"

She made an exaggerated examination of the workroom. "I don't see any at the moment."

"That makes things less complicated for both of us."

She stared at him, and in her eyes he saw the same undeniable attraction he was feeling. After a moment, though, she dropped her gaze to her hands as though it was crucial to get every drop of water off them.

"I saw your recent documentary on public television about unsung heroes," she said.

Sam hadn't been expecting that. But then he should be expecting the unexpected from her by now.

He told himself that it didn't make any difference what she thought of his films. He didn't need constant approval and flattery from everyone he knew, only his own sense of accomplishment.

Oddly enough, though, Brett's opinion did matter to him.

"Is that why you don't want the public knowing about my involvement with Maddox Hill?" he asked. "You didn't like my work?"

She jerked her head up, a shocked expression on her face. "My refusal has nothing to do with your ability as a filmmaker. Your documentary about the women who sacrificed so much, sometimes even their lives, to help runaway slaves make their way north on the Underground Railroad, was very moving and extremely well done. You have to be aware of that. The issue was presented factually but sensitively. The next day I bought a couple of books, to read more about the subject. Your talent as a director has nothing to do with my decision."

"Then what does?" He took a couple of steps closer, ridiculously pleased by her approval. "My staff has checked out the other plantations within a hundred-mile radius of Fredericksburg. Other than Chatham, yours is the only one that fits all my criteria. We will guarantee to do no construction without your permission. A couple of the rooms will be used for a few shots, but most of the scenes will be exterior. As you know, the house was used as a hospital during the battle of Fredericksburg. Instead of concentrating on the military aspects of the battle, I'm featuring a physician who kept a diary during the war."

"Is that how you became interested in the battle of Fredericksburg, from reading the doctor's diary?"

"You're changing the subject."

"Yes. Are you going to answer the question?"

"I might as well. I have a feeling you'll keep nagging me until I do."

"Probably."

He smiled. "I had a grandmother who lived in Atlanta, Georgia. Her family was born, wed, bred, and died on southern soil, as she used to say. She still took the burning of Atlanta personally, and that happened way before she was born."

Brett nodded in understanding. "My grandmother used to point out the hoofprint on a wardrobe door from a Yankee horse. The door had been torn off so the wardrobe could be used as a horse trough."

"I suppose there are a lot of stories like ours," Sam said. "Whenever I visited my grandmother, she would tell me stories of the Civil War and show me a trunk full of artifacts."

"Was the doctor's diary in the trunk?"

He shook his head. "I found the diary along with a bag of medical instruments in a museum in Atlanta."

"His name wasn't Dr. Meade, was it?" she asked.

It took Sam a few seconds to make the connection. "Documentaries aren't the only kind of movies you see."

"I read the book too. *Gone With the Wind* was my mother's favorite book."

"Do you remember the scene in the movie in the railroad yard with all the wounded men as far as the eye could see?"

"Of course."

"I want to show the brutal reality of war by doing several explicit scenes of wounded soldiers waiting to be treated at Maddox Hill. The dramatic impact of uniformed men lying on the ground in large numbers will get the point across much more powerfully than cold statistics."

Brett could easily imagine the scenes he described and felt a twinge of guilt. She didn't like knowing she could be responsible for preventing his vision from being seen.

Sam continued his explanation. "We can't duplicate the exterior of the house on a soundstage or on other land, simply because our budget doesn't stretch that far. But if one of our people leaves so much as a scratch on the floor in your house, it will be repaired. I'll put it in the contract. The tourists who stomp through the place probably do more damage than we would."

"But you would use the name of the plantation in your documentary, which would draw national attention to it."

"Of course." Sam's gaze never left her face, even though her attention was on the towel and not on him as she folded it and draped it over the rack by the sink. "The plantation was part of the history of the battle," he went on. "President Lincoln went to Chatham to visit the wounded Union soldiers there, and I'm going to include that." Something in the hesitant way she looked at him made him ask, "Why does publicity bother you? It's not as though Maddox Hill is a big secret. The plantation is open to the public year-round. Anyone who wants to see it can. I'll just be presenting it to a wider audience."

Brett walked back to the refrigerator to take out more candy. Once she had emptied the molds, she prepared them to be filled again. All the while she did not speak to him, did not even look at him.

Sam watched her. Was publicity all she was against? he wondered. Then why did she have the place open to the public if she didn't want people to know about it?

She took a deep breath and finally turned to face him. "I can't think of a way to say this that isn't insulting, so you'll have to take my word for it that I don't mean it that way."

"You've got my attention."

"You have to be aware that everything you do tends to draw attention from the media. Whether it's because of the Emmy you won or the celebrity women you've been involved with, it doesn't make any difference. The fact that what you do will end up in the newspapers, and possibly on television, is why I don't want you using Maddox Hill in your film."

Of all the reasons she could have given, Sam expected that one the least.

"Let me see if I have this right," he said. "You don't mind if a few people know about the plantation and tramp around the grounds, but you don't want national attention directed at your property. Is that about it?"

"Close enough."

He was no nearer to understanding than he'd been. "Do you mind telling me why?"

She met his gaze directly. "Yes, I do mind. It's private and personal and, frankly, none of your business."

He closed the distance between them in two strides. "That's where you're wrong. Filming Maddox Hill Plantation *is* my business."

"That's not true. You aren't going to film there."

Sam had seen steel beams more pliable than she was. "What can I do or say that will change your mind?"

"Nothing."

"You said earlier that you would think about allowing us to use the grounds. Am I wrong in assuming you've decided against that too?"

"After looking at that option from several angles, I decided it wouldn't be a good idea."

She started to turn away, but Sam grasped her arm to keep her in front of him. She looked down at his hand on her arm, then raised her gaze to meet his.

"Is it so hard for you to accept that you can't have everything you want?" she asked.

"I can accept it, but I don't have to like it. What's going on, Red? Why don't you want attention drawn to the plantation? If you give me a good enough reason, I'll back off."

She shook her head. "I told you, it's personal. I'm not obligated to tell you anything." She tugged her arm out of his grip and walked out of the work-room.

By the time Sam had followed her to the front of the store, Brett was unlocking the door. Frustration clawed at his insides, mixing with fierce arousal as he saw her standing proud and stubborn beside the open door.

Smiling faintly at the defiant tilt of her chin, Sam approached her. He placed one hand on the door over his head and leaned toward her. "You realize I haven't given up, don't you?"

"I wish you would," she said quietly. "It would save both of us a great deal of time and aggravation, and my answer will be the same."

"We'll see," he said, then surprising both of them, he bent his head and kissed her.

He had meant only to give in to the desire to find out how she tasted, but she opened her mouth to object at the exact moment his lips touched hers, and he slipped his tongue inside. In only a few seconds the kiss changed from casual to intense. Sam could feel her heart thudding heavily against his chest. Or was it his own responding to the heated intimacy of her mouth?

He felt himself sinking into a sea of passion that threatened to drown his good intentions. Whatever they had been. He was finding it difficult to think coherently. Her response drove him to drag her hips against his hard frame, the pleasure almost more than he could bear when he felt her soft tummy pressing against his aroused body.

Brett's fingers curled into the front of his shirt as she fell into the passionate kiss, naked longing momentarily overriding her wariness.

When she felt his hand gliding up her rib cage under her shirt, she broke away and stepped back. "That wasn't necessary," she said with difficulty, breathing in deep gasps of air to replenish her starved lungs.

"I think it was," he said, his voice rough with desire.

Sam wanted to reach out for her again. His body was taut with unsatisfied need and his mouth was moist from hers.

"Don't make things more complicated than they already are, Sam," she pleaded.

Hearing his name on her lips had him reaching for her again.

She shook her head. "Don't."

"I'm not giving up, Red."

"I know."

He lifted his hand to run a single finger down the side of her face. Smiling slowly, he continued to look at her, then turned and walked out of the shop.

He still wanted Maddox Hill Plantation, but now he wanted her too. Possibly even more. And certainly for different reasons.

FOUR

By noon the following day, Brett was fed up with hearing about Sam's film company. She was especially fed up with the subject of the attractive director, who had half the women in town getting their hair fixed and finding excuses to be wherever the crew and Sam went. The other half of the female population was under age thirteen and not interested in drop-dead-gorgeous looks and tight jeans hugging a firm male bottom.

Brett had spent a restless night with very little sleep, and all morning she hadn't been able to think of much of anything but Sam and the sensual kiss they'd shared. So she was most definitely not in the mood to chat with her customers about Sam Horne and his entourage's present location in the area.

It didn't help that her assistant working in the shop that day belonged to one of the reenactment groups that had volunteered to be part of the documentary. Brett had to listen to Myra rattle on and on about the friendly producer and the handsome director and what a fantastic opportunity they were being given to be part of an historic undertaking.

During a lull of customers in the shop, Myra continued her saga about meeting the director and the producer that morning. "Mr. Horne should be in front of the camera instead of behind it. The way he described some of the action scenes made us feel like we were right there. You could almost smell the gunpowder and hear the cannon fire while he was talking."

"Mr. Horne is a regular spellbinder," Brett drawled, unable to praise the man who was responsible for her getting very little rest during the night.

"Isn't he, though?" Myra said, taking Brett's comment seriously.

Brett smiled as she looked at her assistant. A plump woman in her midthirties, Myra Overton was comfortably married with twin boys, Stuart and Brent, who owned two dogs, one cat, a rabbit, and five hamsters. Myra could still find the time to appreciate an attractive male when she came across one. Brett couldn't fault her for enjoying the view. Men like Sam Horne didn't come around every day of the week.

In an attempt to get the subject away from the man—he was staying in her mind far too much anyway—Brett asked, "Are you all going to camp out in tents during the filming?"

"Bivouac."

"Excuse me?"

"We bivouac, not camp out. Some of the men will throw down, but we're to set up A-tents for the garrison."

"Throw down?" Brett repeated in amusement.

"It's when the soldiers throw down their blanket onto the ground to sit, sleep, and eat on."

"I remember the last occasion when you, Pete, and the boys spent time out in the woods overnight. You came back with a raving case of poison oak."

"That won't happen this time. Mr. Horne said he wants me to be tending the injured soldiers brought to Maddox Hill after the battle at the Sunken Road. Clara Barton and Walt Whitman were at Chatham with the Union wounded, but the Confederates brought to Maddox Hill Plantation will have Myra Overton." She had been smiling as she shared her excitement until she saw Brett's frown. "What's wrong? If you're worried about me taking too much time off, Mr. Horne said I'll only be in a couple of scenes."

Brett shook her head. "It isn't that. Did you say you met with Mr. Horne and his producer this morning?"

"At breakfast in the dining room of the hotel where they're staying."

"You're sure it was this morning?"

Frowning, Myra said, "Brett, it was only a couple of hours ago. Of course I'm sure. Why? What difference does that make?"

"I talked to Mr. Horne last night and told him for about the hundredth time that I wasn't giving permission for his company to film on Maddox Hill property, that's why. Damn him," she fumed. "He's not taking me seriously."

"It depends on what you mean by serious." Myra looked at her employer for several seconds, then charged ahead. "He asked about you."

Brett started. "What did he want to know?"

Just then the phone rang, and Myra answered it. After taking the order for a personalized lollipop tree, she answered Brett's question. "Mr. Horne said he'd met you, and you seemed like a reasonable woman who would do the right thing when the time came. I'm not sure what that means, but by the look on your face, you don't care for his opinion."

"What else did he say?"

"He and his producer, Darren something-or-other, were interested in the story of how you got your name."

"Myra," Brett said with a grimace, "you didn't tell them, did you?"

Smiling broadly, the woman nodded. "They got a big kick out of it when I mentioned that your mother was a fan of Margaret Mitchell's novel, *Gone With the Wind*, and that your name is a takeoff of Rhett Butler, even though he was a man and you, as we all know, are not. The two men enjoyed the part about your mother wanting to name you Scarlett, but your father absolutely refused and compromised on Brett. Mr. Horne laughed when I told them you have a wimpy bassett hound named Ashley and used to have a nervous kitten you called Aunt Pittycat."

Brett cringed. Giving Sam ammunition for shooting off his mouth wasn't a good idea. He was the type who would use it when least expected.

Picking up the bank deposit bag and her purse, she walked around the counter. "Can you handle the shop for the rest of the afternoon? I have some things to do after I run to the bank. Belle is making deliveries and should be back in about an hour. I'll try to return by four."

Myra waved her away. "I'll take care of things here."

Finding Sam Horne wasn't the problem Brett thought it might be. As she handed over the shop's receipts to the bank teller, she was given the director's schedule for the day, which was apparently public knowledge. Sam and some of his crew were at the Sunken Road with several of the coordinators of the Union and Confederate reenactment groups.

Brett would have preferred to talk to Sam in private, but she didn't want to wait until evening when he returned to his hotel room. Not only did she have no idea when that would be, but Lord only knew how many more people he would tell about filming at Maddox Hill Plantation during the rest of the day. She needed to stop him as soon as possible.

The parking lot behind the national park's visitor center was almost full with vans, trucks, and cars. She managed to find a place to park, and from that spot, she could see a cluster of people standing near the stone wall at the side of the Sunken Road where Confederate soldiers had held their position against the attacking Union army. Nine thousand Union men had fallen during the unsuccessful attack on the stone wall without even one Union soldier reaching it.

Farther up the hill called Marye's Heights, Brett saw one man sweeping his arm toward the stone wall below, evidently describing something to the people standing on either side of him. She was too far away to hear his voice, but not so far that she didn't recognize the man.

She leaned back against her car and crossed her arms over her chest as she watched Sam. Dressed in dark green slacks and an off-white shirt, he shouldn't have stood out from all the other people and the large fir trees around him, but Brett had been able to spot him without any difficulty. If she could only figure out what it was about the man that unsettled her so much, she would be able to counteract it.

"Are you looking for Sam, Miss Southern?"

She turned toward the direction of the low, male voice and saw the man who had been with

Sam the day they had been filming Hugh Mercer's Apothecary Shop. She glanced up the hill, then brought her attention back to the man who stood several feet away from her.

"I found him," she said. "Evidently I chose a bad time to try to talk to him."

"He'll make the time when he knows you're here." Holding out his right hand, Darren introduced himself. "I'm Darren Fentress, Sam's partner in Wild Oats Productions and the producer of this film." He smiled. "I'm the one who's been writing you all those pleading letters about using Maddox Hill Plantation."

Brett shook his hand. "Did either you or Mr. Horne bother to read my replies?"

He blinked in surprise. "Of course we did. Why do you ask?"

"One of you doesn't understand that my answer was no filming would be allowed on my property."

"We understood perfectly, Miss Southern. It's just that Sam has certain visions about how he wants a film to be. As I explained in my initial correspondence, the battle of Fredericksburg will be shown in two episodes on PBS, with a video of the complete series available to the public after the documentary is aired. The first show will cover the preliminary planning behind the battle from the viewpoint of both sides, spotlighting some of the individuals involved, enlisted personnel as well as officers. Sam wants to highlight people rather than battle strategy. The next one will show the fighting at the stone wall, the casualties, the medical innovations that came out of treating the wounded, the heroism, and the drama." He nodded toward the hill. "The battle is what he's working out now with the reenactors so they can work with the stunt coordinators and rehearse the action."

Brett cut him off before he could go into more detail. "I understand what Mr. Horne is trying to present with the documentary, Mr. Fentress. What neither of you seems to understand is that I do not want publicity about the documentary to include Maddox Hill Plantation and neither of you can guarantee that."

"I can prohibit reporters from coming onto your land," Darren said.

Brett directed his attention to a van parked illegally near the entrance of the parking lot. A large logo on its side proclaimed the call letters of a television affiliate from Washington, D.C.

"Everything Sam Horne does makes the news, Mr. Fentress. You of all people must know that. Prohibiting reporters from Maddox Hill will only make them dig deeper for the reason behind the blackout."

Darren glanced at the van. "Publicity is beneficial when we're making a film, Miss Southern. The more press, the more people become aware of the film. We rarely turn down any type of free advertising, so long as it's positive and not negative. Sam and I have high standards when it comes to the type of documentaries we make, but we also have to make a living. The local press would undoubtedly want to feature your property, which would be fine with us."

"I don't care if every camera in the state of Virginia is directed at Sam, you, and your film, Mr. Fentress," she said tautly. "I won't have Maddox Hill and my family splattered all over the newspapers and television screens again."

"What do you mean, again? I haven't released any publicity featuring Maddox Hill."

Brett took a deep breath to try to calm down. "I'm sorry. I didn't mean to shout at you, but if I don't protect my family's rights, no one else will. Seeing Maddox Hill mentioned in the newspapers my father receives periodically will upset him. I want to prevent that."

Darren stared at her intently for several seconds. "Sam didn't tell you I've written to your father, did he?"

Brett felt as though she were sliding faster and faster into a deep pit where the only light was made by flashbulbs, the only sound sirens blaring.

She didn't know she'd swayed until Darren called her name. She opened her eyes, only then realizing she'd made her own darkness by shutting them.

"Dammit, Miss Southern. You're white as a sheet."

"Leave my father alone, Mr. Fentress," she said

tightly. "If you have an ounce of decency, you will let him be."

Intent on getting away from him, she turned to walk around the fender of her car, but Darren grabbed her arm.

"Don't leave, Miss Southern. Sam will want to talk to you. I'm sorry if you don't approve of me contacting Dr. Southern, but he can be a big help to us."

"My father was dangerously depressed after my mother's death, Mr. Fentress. The only thing that saved his sanity was getting away from Maddox Hill and all the reminders of the woman he loved more than life itself. He's finally gained some peace and you want to drag him back to the pain."

Darren swore under his breath. "Sam's going to want my head on a platter. He told me to let him handle any dealings with you. I should have listened to him."

"You would be wise to listen to *me*, Mr. Fentress. Arrange for a message to be relayed to my father by radio and tell him to discard any previous correspondence. Add that his daughter is taking care of everything as she promised." Brett grabbed the front of his shirt in her fist. "Am I making myself clear?"

"Any clearer and I'd have a black eye," Darren said in a wavering voice. "Would you ease up on your grip, Miss Southern? I used to have hair on my chest."

Brett released him and stepped back.

She gazed up at the crowd of people making their way down the hill toward the Sunken Road. Sam must have sensed his partner was looking in his direction, because Brett saw him turn toward the parking lot.

Darren raised his hand and gestured for Sam to join them. She couldn't see Sam's eyes, but she knew the moment he saw her. His gaze was like a caress on her skin.

Sam spoke briefly to the people he was with, then separated from the group to walk toward her and Darren. Her attention was on Sam, and she didn't see the photographer following Sam's progress with his camera. Darren did, however.

"Miss Southern," he said quietly. "Since you have a thing about publicity, I suggest you go to the visitors' center and wait inside. There's a small auditorium where they show a presentation of the battle of Fredericksburg to visitors before they take the walking tour. The room should be empty now. If you'll wait in there, I'll send Sam in, and you can talk to him privately."

Brett caught a glimpse of the photographer and his video camera. She looked back at Darren. "Thank you, Mr. Fentress. I would prefer not to be on the evening news."

"No wonder Sam is intrigued by you," Darren said as though speaking his thoughts aloud. "Most women like all the attention they get when they're with him."

Brett didn't comment. Mr. Fentress had just

given her another reason not to become involved with Sam Horne, besides self-preservation, common sense, and a healthy desire for privacy. The last thing she wanted was to be the center of attraction for gossips and reporters, who to her were often the same thing. She walked away from Sam's partner and went into the visitors' center.

The room Darren had directed her to was dimly lighted with spotlights on a map on the far wall depicting battle lines of the Confederate and the Union regiments. Brett sank down on one of the metal folding chairs in the last row and waited.

The door eventually opened and closed, but she didn't bother looking around to see if the person entering was Sam. She knew it was he. The air around her had become electrified.

He sat down on the chair beside her, stretching his long legs out in front of him and leaning back. He didn't say a word.

Brett had been prepared for one of his demanding questions. When she didn't get one, she glanced in his direction.

His eyes met hers, his expression intensely serious instead of his usual amused manner. For several long minutes they simply looked at each other.

Sam finally spoke. "Darren is a good friend and a damn good producer, but sometimes he forgets he's dealing with people who have feelings instead of bankbooks for hearts. I'm sorry he upset you."

In a flat, unemotional voice, she said, "Tell Mr.

Fentress to leave my father alone, and I'll sign whatever papers you want."

Shock rolled off Sam in waves. "Just like that? Why?"

"You're getting your way, Sam. The whole purpose of contacting my father was to ask for his help in persuading me to change my mind, wasn't it? Well, you accomplished your goal. I've changed my mind. Send the papers to my lawyer's office, and I'll sign them."

Getting to her feet, she turned her back to him and started to leave.

Sam moved quickly to stop her, clamping his long fingers around her wrist. "Dammit, Brett. You can't just announce you've changed your mind and then walk away like that."

She tried to pry his fingers away from her arm. "I could if you would take your hand off me."

"Tell me why you caved in so easily."

She stared at him, fury whirling through her. "Easily? What makes you think this is easy?" Emotion made her voice quaver. "I respond the same way anyone else would to blackmail. I'm making the payoff."

"What the hell are you talking about?" he asked. He brought both hands up to her shoulders to hold her still. "You're crazy, woman. No one is blackmailing or threatening you. Certainly not me or Darren."

"Your partner just told me he wrote to my father."

"He did. But Darren wasn't asking your father to help us change your mind about using Maddox Hill. He was consulting Dr. Southern to confirm some historical facts about the plantation. Since your father wrote a book about its history, we thought he could save us time and energy if we asked him a few things. We need to verify a couple of changes that have been made inside the house. Our research department hasn't come up with whether the wood panels in the great hall were put in before or after the War Between the States. Your father is a well-known historian and lives on the plantation. Who better to check out our information than he?"

Brett stopped struggling. The only thing she was accomplishing was forcing Sam to tighten his grip and making a fool of herself. "Tell your partner to look somewhere else for his facts. I don't want my father bothered with anything involving Maddox Hill."

"Why not? Dammit, Brett, you aren't making any sense."

She knew Sam well enough by now to realize he wouldn't give up until he had the answers he wanted. She decided to give them to him.

"Can you spare an hour right now?"

He narrowed his eyes and looked closely at her. "If it's important, sure. Why?"

"I wish you'd stop asking why all the time. It's irritating."

"If you explained yourself better, I wouldn't have to."

"If you want to know why I've been so intent on keeping you away from Maddox Hill, you'll have to come with me. I can explain everything better there."

"We're going to your plantation?"

"Yes."

With some effort, Sam bit back the urge to ask her what she wanted to show him. This time he would go along for the ride, and not badger her to explain why they were going to the plantation when she'd been so adamant about keeping him away. Perhaps at the end of the trip, he would have some answers.

He didn't even complain when he had to cram his long legs into the front seat of her compact car after he told Darren he would be gone for a couple of hours. Sam hoped they got to the plantation quickly, or he might never be able to walk again.

It was a quick drive, although they were on Brett's property for five minutes or so before they approached some of the outbuildings that had been a stable, a smokehouse, two barns, and a laundry house. A greenhouse had been built about fifty years earlier with the house's original style of construction in mind. A conservatory design had been used rather than a modern glass-and-steel frame. Camouflaged by shrubbery and trees, the brick-and-glass hothouse fit into the general time period.

Instead of driving up to the impressive front

portico with its solid cypress columns, Brett by-passed the circular driveway that was used by the public. She drove along the side of the brown sand-stone mansion, then turned onto a narrow road that ran behind the separate cookhouse and led to the rear entrance of the house. She stopped the car in a small graveled area where two other cars were parked and got out.

Sam did the same, managing to untangle his legs and maneuver his long length out of the front seat without turning into a pretzel. As he walked around the back of the car, he was pleased to be able to stretch his legs. He stopped abruptly when he saw that Brett was staring up at one of the sec-ond-story windows. The look of utter despair on her face made him want to reach for her, to com-fort her from whatever pain she was feeling. The knowledge that she wouldn't welcome his touch right now held him back, and he was surprised by the hurt he felt knowing she wouldn't want his support. Lifting his gaze to the same window, he saw only the reflection of the sky on the glass panes and a sketchy glimpse of dark drapes tied back to allow light into the room.

Brett pushed her private demons aside and glanced at Sam. "Have you taken the tour through the house yet?"

He nodded. "Several times."

She started walking toward the flagstone patio surrounding one of the back entrances. "The area of the house I'm going to show you is off-limits to the public. Unless you and your staff ducked under the ropes cordoning off the private sections of the house, you wouldn't have seen the room on the second floor that we're going to."

Slanting a grin in her direction, he asked, "How did you know we wandered into forbidden territory?"

"Lucky guess," she said dryly as she opened the door and led the way into the house. "The kitchen was originally in the square building we passed. The ladies' auxiliary that maintains the volunteers and the upkeep of the house and grounds has restored the cookhouse so it resembles the original."

They entered a modern kitchen with an assortment of up-to-date appliances and a rectangular wooden table where three older women were sitting with a cup of coffee or tea in front of them. Brett was greeted warmly by the women, who then gave Sam curious glances.

Starting with the lady seated closest to her, Brett introduced Sam. "Mrs. Arthur, Mrs. Pierce, and Miss Norville, this is Sam Horne, the director of the battle of Fredericksburg documentary. I'm sure you've heard of the documentary being filmed in the area. Sam, these three ladies are the backbone of Maddox Hill. Without them, the flowers wouldn't bloom, there wouldn't be any volunteer guides, the dust would be three inches thick on all the furnishings, and the repairs wouldn't be made on the drapes and the linens. Mrs. Arthur lives in the house and is in charge of housekeeping. Mrs.

Pierce and Miss Norville are members of the auxiliary that maintains the house and the grounds."

All three women were on the gentle side of sixty but not too old to appreciate a charming smile from an attractive man. Mrs. Arthur and Mrs. Pierce shook Sam's hand, and Miss Norville, a maiden lady, blushed deeply, shyly extending her hand when it was her turn.

Sam followed Brett's lead by making polite conversation with the three women for a few minutes. If Brett was in a rush to show him whatever it was she'd brought him to Maddox to see, she gave no sign of impatience as the three women engaged her in a discussion of decorations they were preparing for Thanksgiving and Christmas. Unlike many of the other historical houses, Maddox Hill remained open all year round rather than close for the winter. In keeping with tradition, the holiday decorations were made of natural materials available on the property. Miss Norville got into a lukewarm disagreement with Mrs. Arthur about the use of holly over magnolia leaves, and Brett settled the matter by suggesting they use both.

A continuous thumping sound coming from a dog bed in the corner of the room drew Brett's attention away from the women to the dog that was wagging his tail.

"I see Ashley is his usual peppy self," she said.

Mrs. Arthur chuckled. "One of the volunteers said Ashley was frightened by a gray squirrel when he was sitting under a tree. He's been in his bed ever since."

Brett walked over to the large dog bed arranged at an angle in the corner. Kneeling, she cupped the tan-and-white bassett hound's droopy face in her hands.

"Poor Ashley. You're running out of places to go where nothing will scare you." She fondled his long ears and was rewarded by a moist tongue licking her hand. "Yes, I know you love me, Ashley, because you know I make sure you have all your creature comforts like a true southern gentleman should have."

The dog made a whining sound when she stood, but couldn't muster up the energy to follow her when she returned to the table.

Brett made their excuses and led Sam out of the kitchen. When she stopped abruptly halfway down the hallway, he had to put his hands out to steady her as he bumped into her.

"Could you say something next time you plan to stop unexpectedly, or maybe make a hand signal? I nearly ran over you." His gaze switched from her face to her hand, which she had placed on the carved wood paneling that ran the length of the hallway. "What are you doing?"

"Just be patient," she murmured, amusement warming her voice. "All will be revealed eventually. You're going to like this."

She pushed against part of the paneling, and a

scant second later something clicked, clunked, then made a soft dragging sound.

Sam stared in fascination as a hidden door swung open, revealing a set of dark narrow stairs leading upward. His curiosity had him stopping near the entrance to examine the wood carving that contained the mechanism that tripped the catch. He knew the approximate area where Brett had placed her hand, but he hadn't seen which part of the wall she'd pressed in order to activate the door.

"How does this work?"

"I had a feeling this would appeal to you," she said. "We could have simply used the regular staircase, but I couldn't resist throwing in a little drama."

"Throw in some more. Show me how this door works."

Standing on the first step inside the secret passage, Brett reached to the wall on her right. "I'll close the door behind me. Press the only acorn still hanging on the tree that's about five inches from your hand, and the door will open again."

Sam watched as the panel closed almost silently between them. Following her instructions, he pressed the acorn and grinned when the door opened again.

Brett was halfway up the stairs, shining a flashlight beam on the steps in front of her. "I know you'd like to stay and play with the door, but right now I want to show you something while I still think it's a good idea."

Sam had to duck to prevent bashing his head into the top of the small doorway. "How do I close this thing from inside?"

"There's a lever that's located about eye level for me, so it would be chest level for you." Her voice seemed eerily disembodied as she gave him the directions. "Pull the lever down and the door will close. Push it up and the door will open."

Sam closed the panel, but the temptation to play with the mechanism was too strong to ignore. He made it open again. A scene began to form in his mind about how they could use the hidden passage in the film.

A distant voice scolded him out of the shadowy darkness. "Sam, you can play with that later." Brett directed the flashlight on the steps directly in front of him. "You might want to duck your head as you come up the stairs. This passage wasn't built with tall people in mind."

Two seconds after her warning, she heard a thud followed by a muffled swear word. Smiling to herself, she continued up the stairs. One of these days he was going to believe her when she told him something.

"Was this passage built when the original house was constructed or added later?"

"The construction of the main house was started in 1812, but it wasn't finished until five years later because Roland Maddox, the first owner, kept making changes in the plans. He's mentioned in the family archives as being some-

what eccentric, with a generous helping of para-
noia. The secret chambers came in handy during
the War Between the States. My ancestors managed to store some of the family valuables and food
in them before the Union soldiers occupied the
plantation after the battle of Fredericksburg."

Sam was about to ask about the other hidden
passages when he heard the sound of gears grinding softly. Looking up, he saw Brett silhouetted in
a patch of light as another door opened in front of
her. Taking the remaining stairs two at a time, he
was only a few seconds behind her when she
stepped into a room.

Sam watched her walk over to a vanity table
where a number of powders and creams were
stored in crystal decanters arranged on a mirrored
tray. The contents of the containers were probably
responsible for the perfumed scent of the room, he
guessed as he let his gaze roam around the bedroom. There was a closed-in, musty odor under the
flowery fragrances, although the furniture was
completely free of dust, indicating the room was
cleaned regularly.

As Sam looked around the room his attention
was caught by a portrait hanging above the mantel
of the fireplace. Stepping closer, he stared at a
woman who looked back at him with Brett's stunning eyes.

"That's my mother, Melanie Maddox Southern," Brett said unnecessarily. "This was her bedroom."

Sam knew from their research on Maddox Hill that Brett's mother had died the previous year. He hadn't seen a need at the time to investigate Mrs. Southern's death since it didn't have any effect on his filming. Now he wondered if that had been a mistake.

"Your mother was very beautiful," he said quietly.

Brett walked over to him and looked up at the portrait. "Yes, she was. On the inside as well as the outside. The sparkle of excitement you see in her eyes isn't just a dab of paint added by the artist. It's a true expression of her spirit. She had a joy deep inside that seemed to radiate from her, touching everyone who knew her. She used to find pleasure in the simplest things—a walk in the woods in the rain, searching for four-leaf clovers, a drop of dew on a leaf. She made sure whoever was with her saw the same wonder in everything that she saw."

Sam brought his gaze from the portrait to Brett's face. "You resemble her."

Brett shook her head adamantly. "Only a little physically." Turning away, she walked over to a brocade upholstered chaise longue and sat down. "She was aptly named. She resembled Melanie Wilkes in her favorite book, although she didn't think so. My father and I used to tease her by calling her Miss Melly. She would smile and say 'fiddle-dee-dee.' " Brett smiled at the memory, then continued, "I would like to have her sunny disposition and her willingness to see the best in everything and everyone."

"Sometimes nice can be irritating," Sam said as he sat beside her. "Rough can often get more of a response than being rubbed the wrong way with something smooth."

"Maybe," Brett said. "But that wasn't her way. She believed more in honey over vinegar."

"Why did you bring me here, Red?" he asked gently. "What did you want to show me?"

She nodded her head toward the portrait. "I wanted you to see her. She's the reason I didn't want you to bring your production company out here. It would only take one individual moving something in one of the rooms or a reporter digging too deeply to ruin what I'm trying to do."

Sam turned so he could see Brett better. He had a feeling he wasn't going to like her answer, but he asked the question anyway.

"What exactly is it you've been doing?"

Staring at the portrait, Brett said, "I've been trying to find proof that someone killed my mother."

FIVE

Sam's mouth didn't quite drop open in shock, but almost. "What?" Before she could answer, he held up one hand. "Never mind. You don't need to repeat what you said." He got to his feet and took several steps toward the portrait. "It's just that I'm having trouble understanding what I heard."

Brett left the chaise and walked to where he was standing. She stared up at the painting too. "You knew she was dead."

He nodded even though she hadn't asked a question. "Darren had the title searched, and had the record of her birth and death along with a report saying she died here at Maddox." He turned to look at Brett. "She's no longer just a name and a statistic to me now. I'm sorry, Brett."

"Why are you sorry? You were only doing your job."

"I'm sorry you lost your mother. I'm sorry

you're sad, and I'm sorry for being the cause of you having to defend your privacy. You don't want the press to speculate about her death."

"The person responsible for her death thinks he's gotten away with it. He'll be extra cautious if he thinks the press is digging it all up again."

Sam stared at her, a puzzled frown creasing his brow. "You're serious, aren't you? You think someone killed your mother."

"I don't think someone killed her. I know someone did. Another reason for not wanting you and your film crew here is because I'm looking for evidence that would prove that."

"Isn't that what police are for?"

"Their official verdict was that death was due to a fall down the stairs after an overdose of sleeping pills. The implication was that my mother had taken too many pills on purpose, then tumbled down the stairs. The cause of death was a broken neck. Neither my father nor I accepted their theory then or now. My mother never took a sleeping pill or any other type of medication in her life, except for an antibiotic prescribed for an infection shortly after I was born. She believed in natural healing and vitamin therapy."

Sam's gaze returned to the portrait of Melanie Southern. Brett's mother was posed on the same chaise they had sat on, her white dress spread over her legs. In her hands she was holding a book and a fountain pen. The artist had managed to convey the impression that she had just been interrupted from writing in her journal and had looked up, pleased to see the person.

"I can understand how you must feel losing your mother in such a way, Brett. But what motive could someone have to kill her? She doesn't sound like a woman who would have a lot of enemies."

"That same reasoning applies to her taking her own life."

Something was niggling in the back of his mind as he stared at the painting. Finally his gaze narrowed on the book Melanie held.

"Did your mother write something in her diary that makes you think someone killed her?"

"I could have used your deductive reasoning before this," Brett said with a pained expression. "It took me a lot longer to realize the significance of the book in the painting. It finally occurred to me that her last journal wasn't with the others or among her personal belongings, so I began to look for it about a month ago. The fact that I haven't been able to find it makes me wonder what she had written in it that would make her feel she had to hide it."

"Or why someone might have taken it. There is also the possibility she destroyed it herself. A lot of people do. They record their innermost thoughts and feelings, but to prevent anyone else from reading them, they burn the journals."

Brett walked over to a bookcase with beveled glass doors covering the front. She turned a knob in the middle of one of the doors. Using the heel of her hand, she then hit the top corners where the doors joined. They swung open. She reached in and removed a single copy of a series of similar-looking hardbound books.

As she carried the book over to Sam she saw his attention was on the cabinet. She had automatically gone through the usual procedure to open the doors, not thinking of how intrigued he'd be.

He grinned at her. "I bet using the bathroom in this place is a real challenge. Does everything in this house have trick devices?"

"Not everything." She handed the journal to him. "Open this to any page you want and read what it says."

He gave the bookcase one last lingering look, then dragged his attention to the book in his hand. Opening it at random, he read several paragraphs. Melanie Southern's handwriting was small and precise; the few sketches he saw were drawn with a talented hand. Turning several pages, he scanned over the notations and pictures, and the pressed flowers, stalks, and leaves.

"This reads more like a gardener's handbook." He leafed through some more pages. "Or an herbalist's record book. Are all of your mother's journals like this one?"

"Pretty much. The only personal items are when she mentions giving someone an herbal remedy for some ailments and the success rate of each concoction."

"Then why are you so intent on finding her last

journal? Even if you do come across it somewhere, the chances of finding any clues to her death are real slim if she only entered her usual herbal information."

"Because a slim chance is better than no chance at all," Brett said with more defensiveness than she would have liked to hear.

Sam took one of her hands in his. "I'm probably repeating what other people have told you, Brett, but anytime we lose someone we care about, there's always a degree of guilt attached to our grief. Maybe if we'd done this or said that, or noticed something we should have seen, the person wouldn't have died. You have to accept that your mother is gone and get on with your life."

She snatched the journal out of his hands and returned it to the bookcase. "I've accepted her death. I can't accept that she took her own life."

Once she replaced her mother's journal, she closed the doors, hitting the bottom of them with the toe of her shoe, then turning the knob back. If she used a little more force than necessary when she kicked the bookcase, the only harm she did was to her toes.

"Feel better?" Sam asked quietly, close behind her.

"No," she said shakily. "I don't."

He put his hands on her shoulders and turned her around to face him. "Perhaps if you think of something else for a few minutes, it will help. A reminder that life goes on."

Before Brett could ask him what he meant, he showed her.

A variety of sensations blocked out any feeling but deep sensuality as he covered her mouth with his. His hands cupped the back of her head so he could control his passionate assault. He alternated from soft and tender to hard and deep, then back to light, tempting tastes.

Whether it was his intention or not, he was driving her crazy by leading her to the brink of ecstasy, then drawing her back to primitive need.

Sam felt a triumphant joy unlike anything he'd ever experienced when Brett raised up on her toes to press closer to him. Her fingers combed through his hair, her body leaned into his. When he eased his tongue between her teeth, her moan was as much an erotic stimulation as her kiss.

He made a sound of his own deep in his throat as her fingers clenched in his hair and he molded her hips tightly to his. His breath burned in his lungs, his heart rate soared out of control.

She tasted like heaven, and he wanted her like hell.

His hands skimmed over her hips, her waist, her rib cage, up to the curving swell of her breasts. His body shuddered with a hot surge of desire as he ran his thumbs over the tips, marveling at the gasp of arousal that escaped from her.

He didn't understand why, but the realization that Brett wanted him as badly as he wanted her enabled him to release her. He accomplished that difficult task slowly, drawing away from her by degrees to make the withdrawal less of a torture.

This wasn't the time. Her mother's bedroom certainly wasn't the place. He might be having difficulty with the when and where, but not the how. He could imagine making love with her all too well.

Breaking away from her mouth, he eased his hold on her enough to change the embrace from passionate to comforting. He stroked his fingers through her hair and held her head against his shoulder.

He let his breath out in a long sigh. "What were we talking about?"

"I haven't the faintest idea." She tipped her head back so she could see him. "What was my name again?"

He smoothed his hand over her hair. "Red."

"You know, I really hate that name. That's what all the rotten little boys used to call me in the first grade."

"If I had been there, I would have beat them up for you."

"Then you would have continued calling me Red yourself."

He chuckled. "Probably." Moving away from her with more than a little regret, he slid his hand down her arm and clasped her fingers. "Show me how the bookcase lock works."

She shook her head in amusement. "I suppose I might as well. You'll only nag me until I do."

"I do not nag, Miss Southern."

"What would you call it then?"

"Gentle coercion," he said as he walked beside her toward the bookcase. "That's how I plan to persuade you to let me help you find your mother's journal."

She stopped walking and turned to look at him. "Why would you want to do that? I've given my permission for you to use Maddox Hill, so why would you want to help me?"

"Who would have thought there was such a suspicious nature behind that sweet face," he murmured. "Have you given any thought to the interesting little fact that if your mother didn't want to take those sleeping pills, someone had to have made sure she took them?"

"Of course. That's what I'm trying to prove."

"If they've killed once, they might not find it as difficult to kill again. If you're determined to go through with this search, then you have to accept my help. It's too dangerous for you to continue on your own."

"It's been over a year since her death and nothing has happened to indicate anyone is concerned about me or my father finding any evidence of murder."

"Where have you looked for the journal?"

"I haven't accomplished much," she admitted. "I've searched all the rooms on this floor, but it's taken more time to go through each item on the first floor. I can only do my hunting when the plantation isn't open to the public, and I have to put everything back exactly the way it was."

"Tonight over dinner at your place, you can tell me what you've done so far, and who might have a motive for killing your mother. In the meantime show me how this lock works."

"Has anyone ever told you that you are extremely pushy?"

"All the time," he said easily, pleased to see the haunting sadness in her eyes replaced by the more familiar teasing sparkle. "It's one of the many burdens a man of my genius must bear."

She smiled. "I don't remember inviting you to dinner."

He touched her nose with the tip of his finger. "It must have slipped your mind. Are you going to show me how this works or not?"

That evening Brett nearly sliced off her finger as she was chopping vegetables. It wasn't because what she was doing was that difficult. Preparing vegetables for stir-fry didn't require a great deal of mental stimuli, just a little hand-eye coordination.

Waiting for her dinner guest to arrive was the cause of her preoccupation and was responsible for the three onions she'd diced when all she'd needed was one. Though she knew it was silly to be nervous about Sam coming for dinner, that didn't stop her from jumping at her own shadow and wielding the knife as though it were an ax and a stalk of broccoli were a giant redwood tree.

She put the knife down on the cutting board and took several deep breaths, willing her nerve endings to stop vibrating like plucked guitar strings. This wasn't the first time she'd ever had a man over for dinner. Usually she invited them, however, instead of her guests inviting themselves.

Sam would be there in three minutes if he arrived on time. Hopefully, she wouldn't cut off her fingers in the meantime.

Brett took a sip of the wine she'd poured earlier and thought about why she was so tense. It was time to be honest with herself and admit she wasn't sure how she was going to react if Sam planned on more than dinner that night.

After the kisses and caresses they'd shared at Maddox, she knew he wanted more from her than her signature on the dotted line. And Sam had to know that she wasn't indifferent to him either.

Lord, she thought with more than a little embarrassment. She'd practically dragged him down to the floor.

The attraction between them had been there from the very start. She could give it an assortment of labels and file her reaction to him in the casual category of a healthy female responding to an attractive male.

It wasn't simple sexual response, though. What she felt ran much deeper than that. This emotion, whatever it was, was different from anything she'd felt for any man before. *He* was different from any man she'd ever known. And she was different when he touched her. She couldn't even begin to analyze how or why so much was happening between them, considering they didn't appear to have a great deal in common and they hadn't known each other very long.

None of those things mattered, though, she admitted to herself. When Sam was with her, she felt alive in a way she'd never experienced before. And she suspected she wasn't likely to feel like this with anyone else. Lightning had been known to strike twice in the same place, but she couldn't imagine feeling such encompassing need to be with someone the way she craved to be with Sam.

What she had to decide was whether she could accept an affair with Sam, knowing he would leave as soon as his filming was completed and she would never see him again.

When the kitchen clock chimed the hour, Brett went downstairs to the shop instead of waiting for Sam to ring the bell. The only light in the front room was a security lamp in one corner near the ceiling that was directed toward the counter where the cash register was. It was enough for her to see her way around the display tables without bumping into anything.

She didn't need to look through the glass pane in the door to see if Sam was there. Even before she had entered the store, she'd known he was waiting. She unlocked the dead bolt and pulled the door open. The bell attached at the door rang several times, but she didn't hear it.

Sam stood on the threshold holding a lighted candle that was inside a clear glass globe on a brass base. He was dressed in tan slacks and a champagne-white shirt open at the neck under a dark brown sport jacket.

She had changed her clothes, too, discarding her jeans and sweater for a gauzy white skirt and a matching shortsleeve top with a scooped neck. A wide leather belt woven through gold-tone rings was loosely fastened around her waist. She had left her hair down.

Her nerves disappeared like magic when she met his gaze, and she smiled. "I paid the electric bill this month," she said, nodding at the candle.

He glanced past her to the dimly lighted shop. "Knowing that you are naturally thrifty and tend to drag me into dark places, I thought I'd provide the lighting for our dinner."

"How thoughtful," she said as she stepped back so he could enter the shop. "And to think most men settle for flowers or candy."

"No imagination."

"That's true enough." She turned to lead the way to the stairs to her apartment. "Although one gentleman did bring his own silverware, which I thought was tacky."

"Did he have some kind of fetish about eating with strange utensils?"

"You're close," she said. "He was a tad paranoid about germs. When he examined the plate before he put any food on it, I knew we were not destined to grow old together."

She made a startled sound when Sam wrapped his free arm around her waist and turned her to face him. "What's wrong?" she asked.

His voice was slightly husky. "I don't want to hear about other men you've been with." He left a trail of moist warmth as he touched his lips to her throat, the corner of her mouth, her cheek. Returning to her mouth, he murmured, "I don't want anyone else touching you but me."

The abrupt change from casual to commanding shocked Brett. She felt swamped by the fierce rush of male hunger emanating from him in waves. She sensed he was as startled by the sudden shift in mood as she was. Knowing she had the power to affect him so strongly was extremely satisfying to her feminine pride. He was a well-traveled, experienced man who probably could have any woman he wanted. Yet he wanted her.

His name came out low and ragged from her when he broke away from her mouth to sample the soft skin of her throat. Her head fell back and her eyes closed as she absorbed the raging torrent of arousal he was unleashing within her.

She felt a hard edge against her back and realized she was pressed against the counter. He set the candle down on it, then looked at her. She met his burning gaze, seeing her own need reflected there. Mesmerized, she kept staring into his eyes as he bent his knees and fit his hips against hers, pressing into her, leaving her in no doubt as to how she was affecting him. Her fingers clenched in his hair when he buried his face against her neck and groaned, his powerful body trembling with desire.

For her! Brett shivered with reaction, and she knew the decision she'd debated earlier was already made. She could quit breathing more easily than she could resist the passionate call of his need, especially when her own need was so overwhelming, so vast, too extreme to deny.

His voice was rough as he murmured, "Let me inside, Brett."

"You are." Her breath hitched in her throat as his hips again moved against her. "The door is closed."

Raising his head, he looked at her with an expression of naked hunger. "Let me inside you. So hard and deep, I'll never want to leave you."

She felt her knees weaken, and shuddered with a reaction so strong, she felt her consciousness dim. "We haven't known each other very long."

"Your body knows mine very well."

He proved his words by claiming her mouth again in a devastating kiss that mimicked the movements of his hips. Slow, caressing, and seductive, drawing her further into a vortex of passion.

She was so lost in the myriad sensations, she was only vaguely aware of being pulled away from the counter. When Sam slid his right foot between hers, she automatically stepped back, which was exactly what he wanted her to do. She responded twice more to his unspoken demand, but when he slanted his mouth over hers, she became so focused on the pleasure he was giving her, she neglected to follow his lead.

Sam swept her up in his arms and strode into the back room. He spotted the stairs on the far side and didn't hesitate, but carried her up them, his mouth never leaving her lips, her skin.

He stepped into the living room and didn't take the time to ask about her bedroom. He lowered her feet to the floor beside the couch, then gathered handfuls of her skirt until he found her bare thighs.

"You feel like hot satin, Red."

Brett looked up at him. She realized he made her feel proud to be a woman with all the enthralling power of her femininity at her fingertips. It was a gift and a joy that no other man had ever given her, and it created a different need within her, a need to give as much pleasure as she received.

She managed to undo the buttons of his shirt first, then unhook her belt before she slipped her top over her head and dropped it onto the floor. Reaching behind her back, she unfastened her bra and discarded it. The look of appreciation in his eyes encouraged her to allow free rein to her desire to please him. Knowing she *could* please him gave her a thrilling satisfaction. She took a small step forward, which was all that was needed to bring her breasts to his bared chest.

Sam groaned and pulled her into his arms as he took her mouth with devastating hunger. His hands swept over her, memorizing each soft curve, sculpting her breasts and gliding over her waist, her shoulders, and streaking into her hair.

"Sam," she whispered as she slid her hands under his shirt to push it down his arms, yearning and wonder in her voice.

"I can barely stand," he admitted disarmingly. "I'm shaking like a kid on his first date."

He eased her onto the couch and came down over her. His mouth was relentless, never letting up his assault on her senses. Her skirt was tugged up to her waist while he kept her precariously balanced on a tightrope of need. The only way he would let her off would be if he came with her.

Slipping his hand between their bodies, Sam drew her panties down her legs, and nearly came unglued when she arched her hips into his hand, and he felt her moist heat. He cursed the buckle of his belt when his trembling fingers had difficulty unfastening it. Finally he was able to free himself from the confining clothing, although he didn't take the time to remove them, only shoved them out of the way. He cursed his unusual clumsiness again as he tore open the foil packet he'd had enough sense to slip from his pocket.

He slid his leg between hers and was rewarded by the silent invitation of her body as she shifted to make room for him. Sam looked down into her eyes as he hesitated at the entrance of her moist warmth.

"Green fire," he murmured, feeling himself burning in the glow of her eyes and the heat of her soft body under his. "Say you want me. Make me believe it."

"I want you, Sam," she said softly, her hands stroking over his shoulders and her hips lifting to receive him. "I feel like I'll shatter into a million pieces if you don't come to me soon."

Sam's pulse throbbed violently, and he knew he had to take her now or go mad with desire.

He thrust slowly and deeply into her and felt the world spin away. He was drawn into her by a maelstrom of sensations unlike anything he'd ever known. For the first time in memory, he couldn't recognize his emotions. They were too new, too overpowering to analyze. He was losing himself in the woman he'd claimed, and the pleasure was incredible.

Her body was like quicksilver under his, coiling around him with glorious and glimmering pleasure until he was totally possessed as he possessed her.

All too soon the responses of his body were catapulting toward culmination, and he foolishly tried to fight the inevitable.

"No!" he groaned, wanting the pulsing madness to continue. "Not yet."

He surged into her one last time and came apart in a shattering explosion of pleasure and the deepest satisfaction he'd ever experienced.

Brett's body shuddered uncontrollably, and she cried out his name. She clutched him to her as though he were the only thing in the universe she had to hold on to as she went over the edge with him.

SIX

Sam tried to move his arm and discovered he couldn't. For some reason, his neck was stiff, and he attempted to adjust his position to ease his discomfort. That wasn't possible either.

The problem was, his six-foot body was sprawled on a five-foot couch.

If it weren't for the warm glow of satisfaction in the rest of his body, he would have come to the conclusion he'd had a bad night.

He opened his eyes and immediately squinted when a strong light falling across his face nearly blinded him. For a few seconds he was disoriented until he felt a slender leg slide between his thighs. Once his brain started swimming along at a more normal rate, the events of the previous evening came flooding back as though a dam had burst.

He closed his eyes and tried to analyze what he was feeling. It wasn't possible. Too many new emotions were crowded together for him to be able to sort them out and name them. He might be able to fool Brett by pretending their night together was just the result of a mutual attraction, but he couldn't convince himself. Something momentous had happened that couldn't be classified simply as fantastic sex. With her, the intimate act had been much more, had been important in a way he had yet to figure out.

Brett made a vague protesting sound that had him smiling, then he felt her stir in his arms. His amusement changed to a full-blown grin when he opened his eyes and saw a frown creasing her brow and twisting a corner of her mouth. It appeared that his lady was not Little Miss Sunshine first thing in the morning.

His lady? Damn right, he thought. Brett Southern was his in every way that counted. Or would be. He wanted her heart, body, and soul. One down, two to go.

She made another grumpy sound, and he couldn't resist asking, "Do you usually wake up so cheerful?"

He felt her body go completely still. Then she opened her eyes and lifted her head. Since it had been on his chest, she ended up nearly cross-eyed as she looked at him.

He chuckled. "You look surprised to see me, Red. I must not have made much of an impression if you can't remember why I'm sleeping with you."

She closed her eyes and groaned soulfully as she

dropped her head back onto his chest. "Lord, you're one of those people who wake up with the birds and are instantly wide-awake, aren't you? And you're even cheerful about it."

He ran his hand soothingly over her back, enjoying the feel of her silky skin under his shirt. He didn't remember doing it, but he had apparently spread it over her back after she'd fallen asleep on top of him. Since he'd had the presence of mind to see to her comfort, he wondered why he hadn't thought about his own. Her bed couldn't be too far away in the small apartment, and had to be more comfortable than the couch.

When he determined it was possible most of his muscles would work, he shifted to a seated position, skillfully maneuvering Brett so she was sitting across his bare thighs.

Sam was surprised to find he had discarded the rest of his clothing as well.

And all she was wearing was his shirt.

"How do you feel about taking a shower first thing in the morning?" he asked.

"I'm against it. I need a cup of coffee before I can even find the shower. You go right ahead," she said as she pushed against him in an attempt to get off his lap. "I'll make some coffee, which will turn me into a human being after the second cup."

Her movements were having the inevitable effect on him. He nuzzled her neck, aroused even more by the unique scent of her skin.

"You feel incredibly human now." Turning her

face to his, he claimed her mouth with sweet abandon. The fierce urgency of the night before was gone, replaced by a slow-growing passion. "In fact, you feel pretty incredible for a woman." Her skin was soft as satin, as warm as velvet as he stroked her.

She sighed achingly against his lips. "Sam, I don't understand why I have trouble even thinking when you touch me."

"You don't need to think right now. Just feel." He fell back on the cushions of the couch, bringing her with him. "We'll make coffee later," he murmured as he clasped her bare buttocks and brought her against his throbbing body.

Since neither of them had given a thought to dinner the evening before, the delayed coffee was accompanied by a substantial breakfast. Sam insisted on fixing what he called his specialty, French toast, leaving the coffeemaking to Brett. When he asked at one point where she kept her spices, she became curious to see what he was doing. He added cinnamon, nutmeg, and vanilla extract to the beaten eggs and milk, then dipped thick slices of bread into the mixture. The fragrance that filled the small kitchen when he fried the bread made her mouth water.

When their breakfast was ready, they sat at the small kitchen table and dove into the food with healthy appetites. It wasn't until Brett poured them each a second cup of coffee that Sam brought up the subject of her quest.

"I've been thinking," he said.

"When have you had time?"

He grinned. "Have you thought about what you would do when you find your mother's journal? What if you discover it's like all the others she wrote, that there's nothing in it that helps you answer the questions you have?"

"I don't know," she said with a sigh. "I do know that she wouldn't have taken her own life, Sam. You'll have to take my word for it. Right after it happened, my father almost went crazy thinking she'd been so unhappy, and he had been so busy with his work, he hadn't noticed. When he was over the shock of losing her, he agreed that she wasn't the type to take that way out, no matter what problems she might have had. She would search for a solution and not give up until she found it. Giving up wasn't in her vocabulary."

"What about her relationship with your father? Were there any problems in their marriage?"

Brett sat back in her chair and contemplated his question. "I have no way of knowing about their personal life together other than how they were around me." She paused a few seconds, then said, "From my point of view, they were friends in the truest meaning of the word, always able to depend on the other. Apart, they were individuals with separate interests and abilities. Together, they seemed to complement each other, to bring out the best in each other. It's difficult to explain, but I know how devastated my father was when she died. It was as though part of him had died along with her."

Sam knew his next question had to be asked, even though he was sure she wouldn't like it. "So everything was all right between them? There wasn't even a remote chance your mother or your father had been involved in an affair?"

She shook her head. "That was one of the first things the police asked my father. He became furious at the detective. He said he had never once even looked at another woman since he'd met my mother, and he would have known if his wife had been seeing someone else. I believe him."

"They sound like they were close the way my parents are. Last time I visited my folks in Seattle, I caught them necking on the porch swing."

"I thought your family lived in San Francisco."

"My folks moved to Seattle after they retired. My mother's family is there. I've tried to guard their privacy by not talking about them in interviews. I chose the type of work I do, and it puts me in the public eye. They didn't. They prefer the quiet life they have, and I respect their wishes."

Brett felt as though she'd been given a glimpse into Sam Horne's family scrapbook. She wanted to see another page. "What type of work did your father do before he retired?"

"He owned a small neighborhood hardware store and my mother worked with him."

"Are there more at home like you?"

He shook his head. "My parents wanted more children, but I was it."

"Do you see them often?"

"Not as often as I should. Holidays, birthdays, mostly."

She nodded. "That's how it was for me when I lived in New York. My mother told me that I was to get on with my life without looking back. She felt children were on loan to parents, who were to show them the basics of living until they were prepared to go ahead on their own."

He looked at her with the intensity of a laser. "But that didn't stop you from feeling guilty when your mother died, did it? You felt that if you'd been living at home, she might be alive today." He didn't wait for her to agree or disagree. "It would be unnatural if you didn't feel that way. I imagine your father felt the same guilt."

Brett nodded. "I thought he was going to lose his sanity," she said somberly. "He'd been giving a lecture in Georgetown to raise money to save the Brazilian rain forest instead of being home to save his wife's life."

"Which brings us back to the cause of death. What about your mother's physical condition? Would she have told you if she had been diagnosed with an incurable disease or whether she was afraid of growing old?"

"I checked with her doctor shortly after her death. She'd had a complete annual physical three months before she died. Her health was excellent."

"Do you know of any vice or secret she could have had that someone could have been blackmailing her about?"

"Her outside activities consisted of playing golf and doing volunteer work. She spent a lot of time at libraries and plant nurseries doing research for the herbal remedies she made. After Abbie's accident, she visited her several times a week, sometimes taking her out to lunch or just for a drive. None of those activities could even be classed as bad habits, much less vices."

"Would she have told Abbie if something or someone was bothering her? As close as you were to her, she might have been hesitant about sharing something she thought you would disapprove of or wouldn't like her to be involved in."

Brett got up to pour the rest of the coffee into her cup. "After my mother died, Abbie was too distressed to answer many questions. She had finally come to terms with her blindness, only to have her best friend die mysteriously. She asked the same one-word question we all had. Why?"

"She might know something she isn't aware she knows. We'll talk to her. She would want to uncover the truth too. Can you think of anyone else your mother would have confided in?"

Brett shook her head as she sat back down. "My mother had a number of women friends and several men she was on friendly terms with through my father's work, and of course there were people around here they had known and socialized with for years. They spent a lot of time with Judson and his wife, although it was more for Judson's sake. Kathryn Quill has a weakness for bourbon and branch water."

"The attorney with the bad disposition?"

She smiled wryly. "Judson was very fond of my mother and is protective of me. He's usually quite charming."

"Maybe he's more perceptive than I gave him credit for." Sam reached across the table to squeeze her hand. "He must have sensed the attraction between us and didn't like it. But that doesn't help us find a motive for someone to want your mother dead." He frowned. "If she did take her own life, she had to have a damn good reason to do something so drastic. I've run out of ideas."

"Does that mean you believe my mother took her own life?"

He reached over for her plate and put it on top of his. "That means we keep looking for the journal."

She watched as he carried their dishes to the sink. "We?"

"I'm going to be staying at Maddox Hill for the duration, remember? Who better to help you snoop around the old plantation than me? I have a good excuse to be there while we finish the documentary. I can also be on hand if someone decided they wanted to stop you."

"You have your own work to do, Sam. That isn't going to leave you a great deal of free time."

She glanced at her watch. "Speaking of which, I have to open the shop in an hour, and you have a shooting schedule."

He leaned back against the counter and crossed his arms over his chest. His expression seemed oddly distant and cool. "What's the matter, Brett? Are you trying to get rid of me?"

She smiled as she met his gaze. "I don't think that's possible now. Even if you weren't here, you'd be here. Do you understand what I mean?"

His tension seeped away, and he walked over to her. He pulled her up out of the chair and wrapped his arms loosely around her. "I can't recall a single time I've ever been this insecure with a woman. I find I need reassurance that you're as involved with me as I am with you."

She placed two fingers against his lips. "I don't want to hear about the other women you've been with any more than you wanted to hear about other men in my life."

Sam wondered if she realized what she was admitting. In order to feel jealousy, she had to care about him. He was amazed how good that possibility made him feel. An unsettling thought crept in on the heels of that good feeling, though. Was he getting deeply enmeshed in something he might not be able to get out of? Or might not want to get out of?

"When are you returning to Maddox?" he asked, seeking safer ground until he knew where he stood.

"Tonight. I usually spend the weekends there. My two assistants, Myra Overton and Belle Watling, work in the shop on Saturdays, so I don't stay in the apartment on Friday nights. I've found that when I do, I end up in the shop."

"You do your detective work at Maddox on the weekends?"

"Mostly. Occasionally I've stayed there during the week, if business is slow and I don't need to make candy in the evenings."

He planted his hands on her hips. "Do you want some company?"

She met his gaze. "To search for the journal or to stay over the weekend?"

"Both." His thumbs stroked back and forth across her lower stomach. "As for time, we won't be filming much at night. I can be with you then."

"Sam, a friend of mine who does food setups for advertisements and occasionally for feature films has told me what the schedules are like. The hours can be backbreaking when everything runs smoothly and even worse when there are problems. Your film has to be your first priority, not searching for something that might not even exist."

He gave her an odd look. "My priorities have changed since I met you."

"You don't sound too happy about that."

He leaned down to kiss her briefly. "I'm not sure what I am when I'm with you. One of these days I'm going to have to figure it out."

"Or let time take care of it."

"What does time have to do with our relationship?"

"Think about it. Time is the one thing we're eventually going to run out of when your film is completed."

For a man who was known for sticking to schedules and hating to waste time, Sam suddenly wished he could just stop all the clocks. Minutes and hours were ticking away, drawing the day that he would finish the *Battle of Fredericksburg* closer and closer.

Like Scarlett in Melanie Southern's favorite book, Sam decided, he would think about leaving Brett and ending their relationship tomorrow.

He kissed her again. "Help me with the dishes, then we'll get going."

Hours later Brett watched the transformation happen and still didn't believe it was happening. When she'd arrived at Maddox Hill a little after six that evening, there hadn't been any vehicles parked in the space for visitors' cars and buses. Since the house was closed to the public at five o'clock, she would have been surprised to see any, but that was before her agreement with Sam. She had expected to see some of his crew or Darren or Sam himself already there. When he'd left her that morning, Sam had said he was going to round up the crew and send them out to the plantation. She hadn't heard from him or seen him the rest of the day.

She had carried her satchel of personal belongings up to her room, and there she had happened to look out the window. A large van had been pulling up to the first barn. Movement farther up the lane had drawn her gaze, and she'd seen a white truck with the Wild Oats Productions logo sprawled across its side. The truck drove ponderously toward the second barn.

After that, Brett witnessed a steady stream of vehicles of all kinds and shapes. Since none of them came to the house, she felt relatively comfortable taking a shower without fearing some stranger would come strolling in. Ten minutes later she walked out of the steamy bathroom and glanced through the window that faced the meadow behind the cookhouse.

She blinked, then looked again. The reenactors had wasted little time setting up their encampment. Several rows of A-tents had been erected and men in gray uniforms were walking around. She knew from Myra's descriptions of previous reenactments that the men always wore their uniforms, and the women and children were always attired in appropriate mid-nineteenth-century clothing.

Several men had made fires in pits and had set black kettles to one side of the flames. A number of rifles had been arranged in clusters in tepee fashion, their bayonets pointing into the air. Haversacks and knapsacks were on the ground or hanging from tent poles.

Brett marveled at the speed and efficiency of

the reenactors and was beginning to understand why Sam had been so pleased about their assistance.

She walked over to another window and looked out at the barns, where an astonishing number of cars and vans were parked. Like bees around a hive, people were dashing here and there, some carrying wiring, lights, and boxes of all sizes.

She didn't see either Sam or his producer friend, Darren Fentress.

They wouldn't be in their rooms since she hadn't shown them which ones they were supposed to use. Which reminded her, she had better check to make sure the housekeeper had prepared those rooms. Brett had called Mrs. Arthur that morning to tell her about the impending invasion. But first, she'd better get dressed.

Five minutes later, as she was tucking the tail of her dark blue shirt into the waistband of her jeans, she heard footsteps in the hall. She had one sleeve turned up and was starting on the other one when she heard Sam call her name.

Actually, he yelled her name. She shouted back, "What!"

Her door opened almost immediately. Sam stood on the threshold holding a carryall, a look of disappointment on his handsome face. "Damn, you're dressed."

"I thought it was preferable to have something on with your crew in the house." Her eyes widened when he set the carryall inside the door. "What is that?"

"I travel light."

"What makes you think you're going to travel in here?"

He glanced around the room, his gaze stopping at the queen-size canopied bed covered with an antique brocade spread. "I plan to travel as far as your bed later tonight."

"You expect to sleep here?"

"Is this where you'll be sleeping?"

"Yes."

"Then it's where I'll be."

"Sam, you can't sleep here."

"Why not? The bed is big enough."

Brett walked quickly to the window and gestured outside. "What about all those people out there?"

He shook his head and grinned. "There isn't enough room for them too."

"That's not what I meant."

"Darren's fixing up some sleeping areas in the barn for those who don't have their own trailers." He joined her at the window and looked down at all the activity. "Some of the crew have made plans to camp out with the reenactors."

"Bivouac."

"What?"

"It's bivouac, not camp out."

"Whatever. As I told you earlier, we'll need four bedrooms." He named the members of the crew who would use the rooms, including Darren. He didn't mention himself. "You said that wouldn't be a problem."

"I thought one of the rooms would be yours."

He leaned against the window frame and crossed his arms over his chest. "What's the matter, Brett? Are you regretting last night?"

She took a few steps away before turning back to face him. "Of course not. That isn't the issue."

"Then what is?"

"You might be used to this type of thing, Sam, but I'm not."

There was a cool edge in his voice. "Exactly what type of thing are you talking about?" he asked, a cool edge to his voice. "The fact that we're sleeping together?"

"As I've mentioned at least a hundred times, everything you do is news. All I had to do yesterday was go to the bank, and I heard where you were and what you were doing. I had enough notoriety after my mother's death, and I hated the invasion of my privacy, the questions, the innuendos, the rumors. Everyone I know in town is going to have a field day once it's known I'm your latest mistress."

He moved so quickly, Brett didn't have time to react or retreat. He gripped her upper arms and held her firmly in front of him. "I'm thirty-eight years old, Brett. I'm not going to lie to you and say I've never been with another woman, but for your information, I've never had a mistress. I have to put up with the garbage the press prints about my private life if I'm seen with a woman, but I won't tolerate you thinking I'm some sort of sleazeball sex maniac who has to have a lover on every film location."

Brett was astounded to see the hurt expression in his eyes. Knowing she could cause him pain was a humbling experience.

"I'm not ashamed of being involved with you, Sam. Please don't think that. But our feelings won't matter to those people who will enjoy talking about us."

"Our feelings are the only ones that do matter. We can't be responsible for what anyone else thinks or says."

"I know everything you're saying is true. I just had a picture in my mind of the expression on your crew's faces at the breakfast table in the morning."

"People are going to talk about us no matter what we do, Brett. I could sleep in town at the hotel, and you could stay out here, and they'll still think whatever they want, whether it's true or not."

Brett knew he was right. The shock of discovering his intention to stay in her room was wearing off, and in its place was a growing excitement that she could sleep in Sam's arms every night until he left Fredericksburg. She could have a few magical memories to recall after he completed his film and left town. Having to endure a few sly looks and people whispering about her as she passed by would be a small price to pay for the time she could spend with him.

She reached up to touch his face. "I'm sorry, Sam. I guess it was the shock of seeing you put your case in my room."

He placed his hand over hers. "I shouldn't have taken it for granted you would want me to stay with you. But we aren't children, Brett. We don't have to live by anybody's rules but our own. I want to be with you. My schedule during the next couple of weeks is going to be hectic, and about the only time we'll have to be together will be at night. I don't want to give up even an hour of being with you if I can help it."

Brett wished with every fiber of her being that she could believe he was as emotionally involved with her as he was physically drawn to her. Now that it was too late, she wondered how big a mistake it had been for them to become lovers before getting to know each other better.

Taking her silence as consent, he slipped his arms around her. "I should have discussed the sleeping arrangements in more detail with you. I admit that after last night, I had the impression you wouldn't mind repeating the lovemaking we shared."

"So it wasn't just sleeping you had in mind when you put your case in my room?"

He bent his head so he could nuzzle the soft curve of her neck. "Lord, you drive me crazy, Red." He felt her tremble when he nibbled her shoulder, then soothed the spot with his tongue. Lifting his head, he framed her face with his hands. "And it's not just terrific sex, Brett. I like being with you. I enjoy hearing your voice and the comfort I feel when you're in the same room. No woman has ever had that kind of power over me before."

His admission was more arousing than the feel of his hard frame pressed against her. And she had an admission of her own to make. "The way you make me feel scares me, Sam."

"What are you afraid of?" he asked with a puzzled frown. "I'm not going to ask anything of you that I won't give in return. We're good together. We have a number of interests in common. Those things are a good start."

How could she tell him she was very much afraid that she was falling in love with him? she wondered. He'd given no indication that he wanted that sort of commitment from her. Nor that he was willing to give her one in return.

"I've been accustomed to controlling my own life, making my own decisions," she said. "Then you entered my life, smiled that devilish grin, and touched me more than physically. In the span of only a few days, I've not only fallen into bed with you at the first opportunity, I've allowed you and your crew to take over Maddox Hill. I don't seem to know my own mind."

He shook his head. "None of those things are wrong, Brett." He stroked his thumbs across her bottom lip. "I've never felt anything more right in my life. Trust me and trust yourself."

She laid her head on his chest and felt his arms holding her securely against him. If they could only stay like this instead of having to face others and the future.

SEVEN

As Brett turned onto the lane leading to Maddox Hill the following evening, she thought of the difference between coming home to an empty house and knowing Sam would be there when she arrived. She reminded herself not to get accustomed to the warm feeling of anticipation that was tingling through her and quickening her heart rate. The day would come when the house would again be empty except for her dog and Mrs. Arthur.

But they weren't Sam. And Sam would soon be gone.

And she was desperately afraid her heart would be broken.

She glanced in the direction of the encampment as she drove by. The scene looked similar to the way it had been the previous day and early that morning. Men in gray uniforms were walking around the tents, sitting on the ground, or clustering around fires where some women were cooking. People in modern-day clothes were strolling around the barns and equipment trailers. No one seemed to be in a hurry, so Brett concluded the day's filming must have been completed ahead of time.

She smiled when she thought of the shooting schedule tucked away in her purse and the way she'd received it.

When her alarm clock had gone off that morning at six, she was alone in the bed. The only signs that indicated Sam had spent the night with her had been the indention in the pillow next to hers, and the page torn from a memo book that had been left on the pillow, along with a copy of that day's shooting schedule. Underneath a phone number, Sam had written: *This is my beeper number. Call if you need me.* It was signed with the letter *S*, followed by a wavy scrawl that apparently was the rest of his first name. The postscript he'd added had made her smile. *Why can't you look like a hag in the morning instead of gorgeous, tousled, tantalizing, touchable, and . . . Never mind. This is driving me crazy. Later.*

She'd carefully folded his note and put it and the shooting schedule in her purse to take with her.

The other members of his crew who were staying in the house were also gone when she got up. According to the schedule, everyone was to report to the Sunken Road by seven, so the house had been quiet and still when she'd walked down the stairs at six-thirty to make coffee. The only reminder of the extra people staying there was the menu for dinner that Mrs. Arthur had left on the kitchen table for her to approve.

Now, Brett thought as she parked her car, it was evening again and she would see Sam.

When she entered the kitchen, Hank, Sam's head cameraman, was standing next to Mrs. Arthur in front of the stove. He had a dish towel tucked into the waistband of his jeans and was stirring gravy in a deep pan on a front burner. Both he and Mrs. Arthur greeted Brett, then went back to their discussion. Or rather, disagreement.

Deciding this was too good to miss, Brett stayed in the kitchen to greet her dog and eavesdrop. As soon as Ashley saw her, he clumped out of his box and, his long drooping ears flapping back and forth, waddled across the floor to her. She fussed over him, hiding her smile as she listened to Mrs. Arthur recite the ingredients she'd used to prepare dinner, then she declared emphatically that it was not called Yankee pot roast. The recipe had been in her family for several generations, she told Hank, and she would certainly have remembered if any of the women in her family called it a Yankee anything. In a voice that was pure Bostonian, Hank recited back at her his mother's recipe for Yankee pot roast, which did, Brett thought, sound nearly identical to Mrs. Arthur's recipe.

She left them to it and walked down the hall with Ashley plodding along behind her. The dog even made the effort of climbing the stairs to her room, although at a much slower pace.

She tried to ignore her disappointment when she opened the door of her room and found it empty. She had been looking forward to seeing Sam all day, but apparently she was going to have to wait a little longer.

Ashley finally entered her room and crawled under her bed while she gathered clean underwear and showered to remove the sweet smell of chocolate from her skin and hair. Ten minutes later she changed into a pair of tan drawstring pants and a white embroidered shirt that she tied in a knot at her waist.

As she was putting on her shoes she heard a noise above her head and stopped tying the laces to listen. A tapping came from the far corner of the room, up by the ceiling. The sound couldn't have been made by an animal, unless the squirrel or owl wore at least size-ten shoes. Someone was walking around in the nursery, and it was not a child.

The tapping came again, this time about five feet from where she'd heard it originally. After taking a moment to finish tying her shoe, she stepped over to her bedside table and took a ring of keys and a flashlight from the drawer. A hand-woven tapestry covered half of the adjoining wall, and she lifted the edge closest to her and ducked behind it.

The hinges worked silently as she unlocked the hidden door and pushed it open enough for her to slide through. Inside the passageway, a steep set of stairs led to the nursery above. Flicking on the flashlight, she directed the beam to the steps in front of her. She listened for the tapping noises, and at first didn't hear anything but her own breathing. Then the sound continued, louder now that she was in the hidden passage.

When she reached the top of the stairs, she aimed the flashlight toward her feet. The lever she was looking for was two inches from the bottom of the top step and barely an inch away from the wall on her right. Using the toe of her shoe, she depressed the metal lever and heard the grinding of the gears that controlled the panel. She placed her hand on the wall as it swung away from her and stepped around the end.

Inside the nursery, she stopped and stared at the man kneeling several feet away. He stared right back at her.

"Sam?"

"Red?"

"What are you doing in the nursery?"

"Me? How did you get here?"

"You first."

He sat back on his heels and continued to gape at her. Placing one hand over his chest, he said, "You about gave me a heart attack."

"You didn't do mine much good either by knocking on the floor and the walls like some sort of nervous woodpecker. What are you doing?"

He glanced at the bookcase next to her that had moved away from the wall. His eyes were shining with curiosity. "Another secret passage. I'd never have guessed there was more than one."

Brett looked at the metal statue of a Clydesdale horse he held in his hand. "Isn't this a strange time to be playing with toys?"

"I wasn't playing." He stood and walked over to the bookcase, his long fingers searching out the mechanism. "How does this one work?"

"No you don't. First things first. What are you doing in the nursery banging on the walls and why do you have the horse that belongs in the library?"

He took a book off a shelf, leafed through it, then put it back. He removed a few more at random before he was satisfied. They were all real.

"The guy who designed the secret passages was a genius," he said. "Every panel that opens is either decorative or useful. I have to find out more about this man."

"Sam!"

He glanced at her over his shoulder. "What?"

"What are you looking for?"

"The mechanism that makes the hidden door work."

"I mean here in the nursery. If you were looking for my mother's journal, I told you I already searched all the rooms upstairs. You're wasting your time here. I had planned to go over the library next. I'm sure I mentioned that."

He gave her a sheepish grin. "Actually, I was following your instructions. I had started looking through the books in the bookcase opposite the fireplace in the library. I had picked up this horse to get to a book behind it, when suddenly a section of the bookcase swung out and nearly knocked me over."

She smiled. "So you naturally had to see where the passage led."

"Of course. I was doing just fine, too, until I stepped into this room. The secret panel shut behind me, and I haven't been able to find the trick to opening it again. The regular door is locked, so I had to find another way out. I've been knocking on the walls to try to find a hollow section or a lever mechanism that would trip the hidden door."

She held up the ring of keys. "I'll unlock the nursery door and you can take the regular stairs."

He shook his head in mock sorrow. "I don't know why I find you so fascinating, Red. You don't have a single adventurous gene in your body."

"Which is probably why I don't take you seriously."

As she spoke she picked up a coloring book from a stack piled neatly on a toy box. She turned the pages randomly and didn't see the startled expression on his face, or the frown that followed.

Holding the book to the light coming in the window, she said, "I haven't looked at these for years. I stayed inside the lines at an early age, according to my mother." She turned a page. "And wrote my name badly."

Sam wanted to see a sample of her early artistic talents. Peering at the book over her shoulder, he commented, "You also had a fondness for the color pink, or was it the only crayon you had?"

She handed the book to him and began opening drawers in the desk, looking for something. Opening the bottom one, she bent down to lift a shoe box out. She set it on the worn top of the desk and took off the lid.

Sam looked inside. There had to be two hundred crayons in there. "You took off all of the wrappers. How could you tell what color you had?"

She smiled. "And you said I have no sense of adventure." Running a finger over a smear of dried ink on the desktop, she gazed around the room. "I spent a lot of time up here when I was young. I remember drawing different versions of Hansel and Gretel's cottage. The one made of candy and cakes. Some of them were pretty elaborate. When I worked at the hotel in New York, I asked my mother to send the drawings to use as ideas for a centerpiece I created for a children's writers' conference. I was very pleased with the results."

"How did you end up with a career in candy? Most children love eating it, but I don't know any who wanted to grow up to make it."

Brett moved the box of crayons over to give herself room to sit on the desk. "I told you about my mother being interested in herbs." He nodded and she continued, "She was always trying to improve our daily diet, feeding us nourishing food without preservatives or additives. That also meant no refined-sugar products."

"That must have been difficult for you. One of my best memories of my childhood was sitting at the kitchen table after school eating peanut-butter cookies and drinking a big glass of milk with my mother."

Brett shrugged. "I had cookies made of spelt flour, honey, and sunflower seeds. Actually, they were delicious."

"So you didn't feel deprived?"

"Not at all. Chocolate and the royal icing mixtures are too sweet after a lifetime of health food. But since my mother never did any elaborate baking, I was always fascinated by the incredible cakes Abbie used to make in her bakery. She often let Elsa and me play in the back room, as long as we didn't make a mess. As I got older I continued going to the bakery because I enjoyed making things after Abbie showed me how."

"I used to hang out in my dad's hardware store, but I couldn't get too excited about ratchet screwdrivers and roofing nails."

"You got excited about movies instead."

Sam smiled as he walked over to the desk. "Film is a way to communicate an idea, a story, an event. A number of movies entertain or scare people. There aren't that many that educate."

Brett's breath quickened when he stopped only inches away from her. "I think we're back to your curiosity again."

"That's part of it." He placed his hands on her

knees and spread them apart until there was enough room for him to step between her thighs. "I'm curious about a lot of things."

Brett fought the temptation to close her thighs around his hips. "Like what?"

He slid his hands over her thighs, smiling when he heard her gasp. "Like why haven't you gotten married?"

"I could ask you the same question."

"Wait until you answer mine." He stroked his thumbs across the inside of her thighs, enjoying the way her eyes glazed with arousal. "I wouldn't want you to think I'm complaining. I'm damn glad you aren't married, but I find it difficult to understand why you aren't tied to some man with a wedding band."

Brett drew her tongue over her suddenly dry lips, and the movement drew his dark gaze to her mouth. A frown creased her brow as she concentrated on his question.

"I haven't met anyone who wants the same things I do," she said.

"What do you want?"

"He would know."

Sam's eyes raised from her mouth to meet her steady gaze. "You're asking a lot."

"No more than I'd be willing to give."

He brought his hands up to cup her face. "Like friendship, companionship, honesty, loyalty, faithfulness?"

"You left out the most important requirement," she said.

"Love."

She nodded. "Love is crucial and the most difficult promise to make to someone."

"Have you ever been in love?"

"I love Abbie, Elsa, my father and mother, my dog Ashley, and my work."

Something resembling impatience glittered in his eyes. "You aren't going to answer my question, are you?"

"Having an affair with me gives you some rights, Sam. Courtesy, trust, and discretion. But not the right to expect to know my every thought, feeling, and desire."

"Maybe I want to change the rules," he said, a somber expression darkening his eyes.

She put her arms around his neck and leaned forward. "Sam?"

His gaze lowered to her mouth. "What?"

"Shut up."

Amusement curved his lips seconds before he kissed her with fierce possessiveness. His hands closed over her hips to slide her lower body forward to meet his, leaving her in no doubt of his intentions.

She made a soft sound deep in her throat and unleashed the driving need she felt for him. Only him and no one else. She tightened her arms around him as though he was in danger of slipping away from her. As she murmured his name against his mouth she felt a desperation welling up inside her at the thought of the day he would leave.

Sam sensed her urgency, although he didn't know the cause, other than that she wanted him as badly as he needed her. He pressed his hips against hers and nearly lost control when he felt her move into him, seeking the same relief he craved.

Suddenly impatient to feel her skin against his, he wrapped an arm around her waist and lifted her off the desk. With her eager help, he tugged her pants and panties over her hips and down her legs.

His mouth took hers again and again with a passion growing wild. As she sat on the desk again he stroked under her shirt, moaning hoarsely when his fingers touched her bare breast. He shuddered violently as his needs outraced every other emotion.

Except fear.

He was very afraid an important part of him, the center of his being, would be forever destroyed if he couldn't have this woman in his life. Not only now, but always.

He slid his hand down between them to the clasp of his jeans and lowered the zipper.

When he felt her hand push his aside, his breath caught in his throat. She closed her fingers around him, and he buried his face against her warm neck. Whispering her name, he wondered if a man could die of ecstatic pleasure.

"Sam?" she cried softly.

He raised his head and looked into her eyes. "Hang on to me, Red. Don't let go."

Keeping her gaze locked to his, he moved his hips and surged inside her. Her eyes glazed and her lids grew heavy as he thrust against her.

"Look at me," he said. "See what you do to me. Let me see what I do for you."

Her lips parted as he brought them together again and again. She gasped his name as the tension snapped inside her and spun her into a kaleidoscope of colors and sensations. She held on to his back as he shuddered violently and thrust once more in an explosion of indescribable pleasure. He dropped his head to the curve of her shoulder, and she shut her eyes tightly.

Sam's arm held her in an unrelenting grip, locking her to him as they slowly regained their equilibrium.

Brett had no idea how long they had been in the nursery, nor did she care. Everything important in her life was here. She needed nothing or no one else but Sam Horne.

All too soon sanity returned and, with it, the knowledge of other people in the house, other responsibilities.

Sam marveled at the difficulty he had with the simple act of raising his head, which felt as weighed down as his arms. If he had a choice, he would have chosen to stay where he was for the next century.

"This has never happened to me before," he said.

"What?" she asked.

"I'm speechless."

She smiled. "That won't last long."

Sighing, he moved away enough to adjust his clothing. Then he bent down to retrieve her pants and panties.

When Brett realized he was prepared to help her get dressed, she held out her hand for her clothes. "I'll do that," she said.

He held the panties out of her reach. "This is research."

His remark was so unexpected, she simply stared at him.

"I want to see," he explained, "if helping you get dressed is as exciting as taking your clothes off."

She acquiesced, feeling a little like a Barbie doll as Sam lifted first one leg, then the other to slip on her panties. He repeated the procedure with her drawstring pants.

"Well?" she asked as he tied a bow in the drawstring. "What's the verdict?"

"There's no contest." He leaned forward to kiss her with a lingering remnant of passion on his lips. "Removing your clothing wins hands down."

She smiled and slipped her arms around him to hug him.

Sam clasped her to him, holding her, his throat suddenly choked with emotion.

She broke away first. "We'd better make an appearance or your crew is liable to call out a search party."

"I suppose," he said with honest regret. "I'm going to watch carefully what you do to get us out of here. I'd like to come back with you sometime."

"Bring the metal horse with you."

She walked up to a set of brass candle sconces set into the wall on either side of the bookcase he'd been examining when she had surprised him. She turned the one on the right ninety degrees to the left, and turned the one on the left ninety degrees to the right. The slow crawl of chain and gears was the only sound in the room as one end of the bookcase moved away from the wall.

Brett left the nursery first. Sam entered the passage and was about to ask how to close it when the panel slid shut on its own.

After they'd descended to the first floor, Brett put a finger into a hole in the wall to press a lever hidden inside. The door opened to reveal the library.

Brett was showing Sam how to replace the horse in the slots on the shelf when Darren walked in.

"I should have figured you'd be in the library, Sam. I looked for you everywhere else."

"Any particular reason you wanted to find me?"

"Mrs. Arthur just told me dinner is ready, and Hank announced we're having Yankee pot roast.

We'd all better go in to eat before whatever it is ends up on the floor."

Sam grinned and held his hand out toward Brett. It was the first time he had touched her in front of anyone else.

Meeting his gaze, she grasped his hand.

EIGHT

The crystal prisms of the chandelier that hung in the foyer of her lawyer's office swayed and crashed into one another when Brett slammed the door. Judson Quill might have been her parents' close friend and a competent attorney, but he was not her keeper. He had no right to tell her how to live her private life.

As she had predicted, during the past several days the word had gotten around that Sam Horne was staying at Maddox Hill Plantation with Brett. Belle had mentioned to her mother that Brett hadn't spent Monday night at the apartment above the store. Belle's mother happened to tell her canasta club, and soon the gossip had spread faster than the measles in a kindergarten class.

When she had come to work that morning, Myra had teased Brett about Sam, but she didn't overstep the boundaries of their friendship by insinuating the relationship was doomed, nor did she give advice about how Brett should handle her personal life.

Judson Quill had done both.

Brett had called on Monday to make an appointment with Judson. She wanted to tell him she had changed her mind about Sam's company using her property for his documentary, and ask Judson to go over the papers she had to sign. His secretary had told her Judson had a full schedule until late Wednesday afternoon.

She knew Judson would disapprove of her decision to allow the property to be used, but she hadn't expected him to react so strongly against Sam and some of his crew staying at the mansion. That fact seemed to bother him more than the vast numbers of reenactors, actors, and other crew members who were using the grounds of the plantation.

And that was before she mentioned she was staying in the house too. Then he totally lost all pretense of handling her case as a professional. He became very personal.

He went too far when he accused Brett of debasing her mother's memory by cohabitating with a man under Melanie's roof. Brett didn't bother denying her relationship with Sam, although she did point out that her personal life was none of Judson's business.

Judson hadn't listened to her, but had started telling her about Sam's past associations with other women, surprising Brett with his knowledge of Sam's personal history. When she asked him about it, he further infuriated her by telling her he'd been collecting information for a file on Sam.

She had stormed out, which hadn't accomplished anything, but it had given her the satisfaction of disrupting the serenity of his office by slamming a few doors.

She was still fuming about Judson's actions when she arrived home that evening, but tried not to show it. She only had enough time to shower and change before dinner, and no opportunity to talk to Sam. When she walked into the formal dining room, everyone else was already there. She took her seat at the head of the table, opposite Sam.

Hank sat on her left, nearest the kitchen door. Brett had noticed he spent most of his spare time in the kitchen. Mrs. Arthur had frowned at first and mumbled about the nuisance of having a man cluttering up the kitchen. That morning, however, Brett had been amused to see that Mrs. Arthur smiled continually and blushed whenever Hank spoke to her.

Beside Hank was his assistant, Wade Hamilton, who resembled a highly nervous bantam rooster. He had red hair and a quick speech pattern that reminded Brett of a record playing at a fast speed.

On the other side of the table were Darren and his assistant, Terry Cummings. Terry was an attractive blonde whom women wanted to dislike when they learned she could eat her weight in chocolate éclairs and never gain an ounce. But as soon as Terry smiled and spoke to a person in her generous and warm way, it was impossible not to like her.

As usual, Terry and Darren kept the dinner conversation rolling along at a fast clip with good-natured bantering. Brett was just as glad to let the others talk, half listening as they discussed how the day's shooting had gone.

By the time everyone was cleaning their plates, she was rather pleased with herself that she had managed to cover up her anger.

Or so she had thought.

"If you hold that wineglass any tighter, Red," Sam said out of the blue, "you're going to break the stem. Did you have a bad day?"

Brett didn't play the game of denying something was wrong. She always tried to be as honest with her feelings as she expected other people to be about theirs.

Nodding to Darren to include him in her answer, she said, "There might be a delay in the paperwork giving Wild Oats Productions permission to use Maddox Hill."

Darren reacted first. "Why? Have you changed your mind?"

She shook her head. "But I may have to change lawyers."

Sam's gaze narrowed as he leaned back in his chair. "What did Quill say to you?"

"We were supposed to have a meeting of the

minds, but Judson lost his somewhere along the way."

"What did he say?"

Brett could feel her cheeks growing warm as she recalled the accusations and implications Judson had made.

"Brett?" Sam prodded when she didn't say anything.

"I didn't enjoy hearing what he said the first time. I certainly don't want to repeat any of it." She smiled weakly. "I had the last word only because I stormed out of his office."

"Did you shut the door in Miss Frostbite's face?" Sam asked.

"His secretary wasn't around." Her eyes gleamed with satisfaction. "But I made the chandelier clatter like crazy when I slammed the front door with everything I had."

"That's my girl," he said with pride, as though she'd just won a Pulitzer Prize. "Don't worry about the papers. Darren can call Carl Trenton, our attorney in San Francisco, to go over anything you want explained. We'll set up a conference call and leave Judson Quill out of it."

Darren looked from Sam to Brett, a puzzled frown between his eyes. "I wonder if your attorney is any relation to this dingbat lady who keeps nagging Terry." Turning to his assistant, he asked, "Terry, didn't you say her name was Quill?"

Terry had just taken a forkful of cooked yellow squash, so she settled for a nod as a reply.

"What is she pestering Terry about?" Sam asked.

Terry was finally able to speak. "This woman wants a part in the documentary. And not just a walk-on. She wants a starring role. She insists she has had 'extensive training in the arts,' as she puts it."

"Don't they all," Darren said. "Remember that guy who had gotten his picture in the paper for pumping gas into the car belonging to the fiftieth customer and thought he should be in the 'movin' pikchurs'?"

Terry nodded. "That's about the size of it. This woman's experience consists of a few parts in local theater productions. Apparently, she has a costume left from her role in *The King and I* that she wants to use for our film." Terry grinned at Sam. "She dragged this dress, that had about ten yards of material in the skirt alone, along with her and showed it to me. Deborah Kerr would have laughed herself silly if she could have seen it. I doubt if any self-respecting southern woman would have been caught dead in that gown in the 1860s, or any other time period."

Hank took exception to Terry's remark. "There were loose women in that time period, just like any other."

"I bet you didn't learn that in high-school history class," Terry said.

"My dear child," Hank replied, "there have been loose women since the beginning of time."

"Actually," Brett said, "that term was used to describe shameless women who went without their stays. When they weren't properly cinched into their undergarments, they were considered loose women, literally and figuratively."

Terry nodded her head vigorously. "This Quill woman definitely has something loose, and it's not her underwear."

Hank and Wade laughed. Sam looked at Brett. "Do you know her?"

"It has to be Kathryn, Judson's wife. Actually, she's his second wife. My mother always felt sorry for her because Judson's first wife was a hard act to follow. The first Mrs. Quill has become something of a saint with each passing year that her friends have had to deal with Kathryn. According to my mother and father, Judson has spent a lot of energy smoothing over some of the feathers Kathryn has ruffled. My mother felt Kathryn basically tries too hard to fit into the role of Judson's wife, whereas if she relaxed a little, people would accept her as herself and not as a substitute for Judson's first wife." Turning to Terry, she added, "Please don't feel you need to find a role for her just because she was a friend of my mother's."

Terry smiled. "Don't worry. I won't. I told her that all the roles have been cast, but we would call her if we could use her as an extra in any of the crowd scenes. She said not to bother. Then she asked about stand-ins for the actors. I told her they had also been cast. Then she wanted to know what would happen if the understudy became sick at the same time as the actor they would stand in for."

"Maybe we'd better hire a food taster," Darren said. "It doesn't sound like this woman is going to give up."

Sam pushed his chair back abruptly. "If you'll excuse us, Brett promised to show me her mother's greenhouse."

That was news to Brett. She went along with the excuse he'd given, though, since she had a pretty good idea why he wanted to speak to her alone. She couldn't help but notice the grim lines around his mouth after she'd mentioned her meeting with Judson. They were still there, along with a determined glint in his eyes. He would want to know exactly what Judson had said to her. She was learning that Sam Horne was big on details, and not just when it pertained to his work.

She pushed back her chair and was about to excuse herself when the swinging door connecting the dining room to the kitchen was violently pushed open and crashed loudly into the sideboard beside it. Everyone turned toward the doorway as a man burst into the dining room.

His gray uniform made it obvious he was one of the reenactors. "Mr. Horne," he said, looking immediately at Sam. "You'd better come quickly. There's a fire in barn number one."

Darren's chair toppled over as he jumped to his feet. "That's where we stored the camera equipment."

Sam was running for the door when he said over his shoulder, "Brett, call the fire department."

Brett raced to the nearest telephone, which happened to be in the kitchen. Everyone else who had been in the dining room followed Sam through the kitchen, slamming the outside door as they headed toward the barn.

Her heart was lodged in her throat at the thought of all of them running into danger, but Brett managed to give the vital information to the person who answered the emergency number. When she hung up the phone, she saw Mrs. Arthur wringing her hands as she looked out the kitchen window, murmuring under her breath, "Oh, dear. Oh, dear."

Brett approached the older woman and put her hand on her shoulder. "The fire department is on its way, Mrs. Arthur."

She glanced past the housekeeper to look out the window. The sky was dark with only a half-moon providing any natural light. She could see pairs of car lights moving toward the barn as the alarm went out and the crew arranged the cars so their headlights were directed at the barn. There were also a few security lights attached to the building; her father had installed them on all the outbuildings for insurance purposes. Flashlights danced back and forth across the field from the encampment as more people ran toward the barn.

Brett strained her eyes to see any sign of fire coming from the large structure. The lights inside the barn flashed on, and it was then she could see a thin column of smoke rising from the upper door of the hayloft. Then flames licked the dark sky, and gray smoke was caught in the beam of a security light attached to the arch in the barn roof.

"Will you make some coffee, Mrs. Arthur?" Brett suggested, more to keep the housekeeper busy than out of a genuine need. "I have a feeling it's going to be a long night."

"Of course." The older woman visibly pulled herself together. "I should have thought of that myself." When she saw Brett walking toward the door, fear was back in her voice. "You aren't going out there, are you, Miss Brett?"

"I have to, Mrs. Arthur. This is my family's land and it's my responsibility to take care of it."

And she had to make sure Sam was all right, but she didn't admit that to the housekeeper. She was frightened enough just thinking about something happening to Sam without putting it into words. Thoughts spoken aloud gave them power, and Brett didn't want to make her fear any stronger than it already was.

Once she was outside, she could smell the acrid odor of smoke and see orange flames reaching into the darkness. Far off in the distance, she heard the faint scream of a siren. A little of her fear receded. The fire department would be there soon.

She ran toward the barn. Men in gray wool uniforms worked beside men in casual modern clothes as they hurried in and out of the barn, giving the scene an eerie otherworldly view. Each man went into the barn empty-handed and exited carrying equipment, moving quickly and efficiently like a team of ants.

Occasionally someone would yell a warning or an order to do something, but the sound overpowering everything was the ominous crackle and snap of the fire in the loft of the barn.

Brett ducked around the lines of men and entered the barn. She recognized several familiar faces of crew members she'd met during the last several days, even though their faces were blackened with smoke. Then she spotted Darren directing people as they carried the valuable cameras and other pieces of equipment out of the barn. Darren's tan shirt was soiled with smoke and grime, his face smudged with sweat.

A gray haze hung in the barn, making the air heavy and pungent. Looking up, Brett couldn't see any flames coming through the floorboards of the loft overhead. She hoped that meant the fire was contained there and wouldn't spread to the rest of the barn.

Suddenly something crashed onto the floor above, sending angry red-and-yellow sparks through the cracks. Five men moved quickly from beneath the area as water started falling between the boards.

Someone had hooked up a hose to the barn's water supply, she realized. A green length of hose stretched across the floor and trailed up the ladder leading to the loft.

Some idiot was in the loft fighting the fire with a garden hose!

She bit her lip as panic clawed in her stomach. Where was Sam?

She made her way through the lines of men until she reached Darren. "Where's Sam?" she asked anxiously.

Darren hefted a large carton off the floor and handed it to the next man. When his hands were free, he jabbed one thumb in the direction of the loft. "He's checking out the fire with Hank." He gaped as she whirled around and pushed through the men, heading toward the ladder to the loft. "Dammit, Brett!" he yelled after her. "Don't go up there. It isn't safe."

She looked back at him. "Then Sam and Hank shouldn't be up there. I'm going to get them down. The barn can be replaced. They can't."

"If you get hurt," Darren yelled as she scurried up the wooden ladder, "Sam will hurt me. Keep that in mind and be careful."

"If he's hurt and you didn't try to stop him, I'll do more than hurt you," she shouted back.

"I can't win," Darren muttered.

"You never can with a woman," said the man who was next in line, waiting for Darren to give him something to carry out. "Maybe I should set up the video cam," he went on. "Everyone would like to see the fireworks go off when a woman tells Sam Horne what to do."

Darren didn't answer at first. He watched as Brett paused halfway up the ladder, staring at something on one of the rungs. Whatever it was, she plucked it off and shoved it into her jeans pocket. Then she disappeared into the loft.

"If anyone can do it, I bet she can," Darren finally said.

"You're kidding, right, boss?" the man said. "This is Sam Horne we're talking about."

"Even a mighty oak can get cut down, Shorty." Darren pointed toward a number of containers that were marked FRAGILE. "Get some men to help with the spare lights. Put them somewhere where they won't be crushed by someone who doesn't know what they are. The bulbs will all probably have to be cleaned."

Shorty glanced once more toward the loft, shrugged, and did as he'd been told.

Sam spotted Brett the second her head and shoulders cleared the floor of the loft.

"Dammit, Brett!" he yelled.

He shoved the hose toward Hank, then strode across the loft to her, reaching her as she stepped off the ladder and took several steps toward him. He immediately turned her around.

"What the hell do you think you're doing? Climb back down that ladder before you get hurt."

His order lost some of its impact when he coughed. Water pouring on charred wood had created a smudge-pot effect. The smoke was so thick, it seemed solid in places.

Brett gasped for air and coughed harshly when she breathed in mostly smoke. Her eyes began to tear from the acrid fumes, which made Sam curse when he was finally able to catch his breath.

"Do you have some kind of death wish I should know about?" he asked.

"Don't be ridiculous," she said angrily, wiping her sleeve across her eyes.

The sight of her face already streaked with smoke and tears made his throat ache. Taking her arm, he drew her back toward the ladder, his gaze on the floor. It seemed safe enough in this part of the loft. When she tried to pull away from him, he tightened his fingers around her arm.

"Sam!" she yelled. "Look out!"

He twisted his head around and saw a burning board break away from the side of the barn and begin to fall toward them.

Wrapping his arm around her waist, he pushed her, following her onto the floor to roll with her several times. Red-hot embers flew into the air as the board fell.

Hank doused the area with water. "Sam, you and Brett all right?"

"Yeah. We're okay."

Sam levered his long frame off Brett and got to his feet quickly, ready for any other surprises. Everything seemed safe, so he pulled Brett to her feet. He didn't realize his hands were shaking until she was standing in front of him. He searched her face for any signs of pain.

"Don't ever scare me like that again, Red. I lost ten years off my life."

"You're welcome."

"What?"

"If I hadn't warned you, the board would have hit you. Yelling at me is evidently your odd way of thanking me."

"I'm yelling at you because you shouldn't be up here in the first place, and I'm going to continue yelling at you until you get your charming little butt down that ladder."

"The fire is almost out," she pointed out. "Look. Hank is soaking down the last few flames."

"Fire or not, I want you down that ladder. Some of this flooring is burned straight through."

"Only if you come too," Brett said stubbornly.

His clothing smelled of smoke and his hands and face were grimy with soot, but he looked wonderfully alive. She wanted him to stay that way.

"We're almost through up here," he said. "I'll be down in a minute."

She crossed her arms over her chest. "I'll go when you do."

Sam was about to raise his voice to order her to do as he asked when he looked closer and saw the haunting fear in her eyes. Fear for him? he wondered. He felt his chest tighten with an unfamiliar emotion. Suddenly he needed to touch her physically, a response to the way she had touched his soul.

He was so stunned by his own emotions, he could barely speak above a hoarse whisper. "I couldn't take it if anything happened to you, Brett. Please go back to the house where you won't be hurt."

Her eyes were awash with tears as she looked up at him. "What makes you think I won't be hurt if you get injured or worse?"

He stared at her, then pulled her into his arms. He held her so tightly, she could barely breathe, but she didn't resist, holding him almost as fiercely.

Suddenly red lights flashed across the loft like a flickering silent movie. The fire trucks had arrived. Thankfully, the sirens had been cut off before they reached the crowded area. There was enough chaos without adding earsplitting noise.

Sam took Brett's hand and brought her along with him, away from the ladder for a change. "Watch where you step," he said as he stopped beside Hank.

She glanced at the gaping hole surrounded by blackened wood where the loft flooring used to be. The strong odor of kerosene and wet straw made her wrinkle her nose. A bundle of partially burned straw had been kicked away from the area. She frowned when she saw the straw. The loft was supposed to be empty.

Realizing what she'd unconsciously concluded, she looked at Sam with wide, puzzled eyes. "Someone started this fire on purpose." When he nodded, she asked, "Why?"

Firemen clambered up the ladder and began to fill the loft, instructing the "civilians" to vacate the premises. One of the firemen actually said "vacate the premises." Brett suppressed the desire to laugh. No one else would think it was funny.

She chanced a glance at Sam and caught the twitch at the corner of his mouth. She looked away and "vacated" down the ladder. He and Hank followed.

The firemen had cleared everyone from the barn. Outside, Darren was arguing with a fireman that all the equipment hadn't been removed, but he was still not allowed to go back in.

As she watched the firemen do their job Brett shook her head in bemusement. "Why would someone set fire to the barn?" she asked Sam again. "The only thing of any value is your film equipment." She met his gaze. "I just answered my own question, didn't I?"

He nodded.

During the next half hour, Brett remained at Sam's side as he described to the firemen what he and Hank had found when they had climbed up into the loft. Luckily, Hank had remembered seeing a water hose coiled on the floor of the barn near the empty horse stalls. He'd quickly turned on the spigot full blast, and they were able to control the blaze before it spread very far. If the straw had been dry, they might not have been able to contain the fire. As it was, the damp straw had created a great deal of smoke, which might have been what the arsonist had wanted. Or else, the arsonist wasn't very smart.

A police car arrived shortly after the fire trucks, and even more questions had to be answered. Brett was asked about the contents of the loft, and she explained that the barn had been mostly empty. Her father had sold off the horses after his wife had died and the barn had been totally cleaned out to be used for storage of mowing equipment and other lawn and garden supplies. The loft had been completely bare. The straw had to have been placed there by whoever had started the fire.

When asked if she had any idea who could be responsible for the arson, Brett edged around the truth. "I don't know why anyone would want to burn down the barn."

The policeman jotted everything down in his notebook, then asked about the amount of fire insurance she had.

She felt Sam stiffen beside her and placed her hand on his arm as she answered. "As this is an historical home, no amount of insurance would be adequate to replace any building that is lost. Feel free to check the policy on file in my lawyer's office." She gave him Judson's address, adding calmly, "You might also like to check my property tax records, which are fully paid, and my bank account balance. You'll find I have no reason to burn down my barn for the insurance money."

The policeman glanced at Sam, who still stood tense and rigid beside Brett. "We have to ask these questions as a matter of routine, ma'am, to eliminate the obvious."

"I understand. As I said, feel free to check whatever is necessary. I have nothing to hide."

The policeman turned to Sam, looking as though he would rather eat live bait than interrogate the unsmiling director. He bravely carried out his duty, and after noting Sam's answers, however curt, he moved on to talk to some of the men who had been on the scene from the time the first alarm had gone out about the fire.

Finally, the fire trucks departed, followed shortly by the police car. The crew members returned to their trailers, the reenactors to their tents. Sam took Brett's hand in a firm grip and walked back to the house. Instead of going into the dining room, where Mrs. Arthur had set up a coffee urn, he drew her along with him toward the stairs. Brett had to practically run to keep up with him as he took the steps two at a time.

He didn't speak at all as they walked down the hall to her room. He pushed the door open, then with a hand at the small of her back, ushered her into the room. Once inside, he kicked the door closed and pulled her into his arms.

Leaning back against the door, he buried his face in the curve of her neck. He inhaled her fragrance, the spicy floral perfume she wore and the unmistakable scent of smoke and her skin. He was as fragrant as the fires of hell, but she smelled like heaven.

"Don't ever do that to me again," he said.

She wrapped her arms around his neck, startled by the intensity of his voice. "Do what?"

"Don't ever scare me like that again."

"Sam, I wasn't in any more danger than you were. You had everything under control by the time I got to the barn."

"You're wrong. I didn't have myself under control when I looked up and saw you in that loft. I had just gotten my balance after stepping on a weak part of the floor. If Hank hadn't grabbed my arm, I would have gone right through and crashed to the ground. I felt sick to my stomach when I thought of that happening to you."

"It didn't." She loosened her arms from around his neck and stroked her fingers over his chest in a soothing motion. "I'm fine, and so are you. The only thing damaged is a few feet of boards, which won't be that difficult to repair."

Sam refused to be placated by her tender touch and soft words. The fear of something horrible happening to Brett was still clinging to his thoughts like a bad dream, and he couldn't dislodge it. His hands began to move over her as though he needed physical proof that she was all right.

He relished the feel of her curved thighs, sloping hips, and proud breasts. When she gasped at his caresses, he absorbed the sound along with the delicious feel of her firm body under his hands. No one had ever brought him to the brink of desire as fast as she did. Nothing had ever felt as good as she did against him, under him, around him.

The need to claim her, to possess her, was raging through him, making his hands shake as he started tugging at her clothing. He unzipped and unsnapped her jeans, then dragged them and her silk panties down her incredible legs.

She stepped out of them and drew her hands down his chest to the waistband of his pants. She locked her gaze with his as she lowered the zipper and slid her hand inside his jeans.

Sam groaned when he felt her warm fingers curl around him. "Brett," he said roughly, "you make me burn so hot. I feel like I'll explode."

The role of aggressor was unfamiliar to Brett, yet she loved knowing she could make him respond so passionately to her touch. She loved the feel of him.

She loved him.

Her body trembled in response to her silent admission, and she leaned against Sam, needing to be closer to his warmth. While she still could. The thought of him leaving for good fed her desperate need to meld with him as intimately and as long as possible.

Sam felt her desire in her touch, in the way she stroked her hands over him. Placing his own hands under her thighs, he lifted her, then brought her down on him, joining them. For a few moments he simply savored her heat consuming him. Then

Brett pressed her thighs into his hips and rose and fell on him until he felt his consciousness dim. He groaned her name as he moved against her, again and again. Her name escaped his lips when she responded with an exquisite, erotic grace that hurled him into a whirlpool of white heat.

His hands tightened on her hips as tremors of satisfaction and a pleasure so extreme, he thought he would surely die from it, rippled through him to his very soul.

Brett cried out as the coiled tension deep inside her snapped, and she toppled into a shimmering darkness. Her eyes closed, her arms holding Sam in a fierce hold, she let the passion claim her.

Sam leaned heavily against the door, feeling incredibly weak, yet strong and invincible. He nearly groaned aloud when he felt the sweet spasms within Brett caress him.

The only sounds in the room were the faint ticking of the bedside clock and their raspy gulps of air, gradually slowing to a more normal pace.

Unable to bear the thought of parting from her, Sam held Brett tightly locked to him as he walked over to her bed. The movement of her body on his as he covered the short distance had him fully aroused again by the time he reached the bed.

He laid her on her back and followed her down, his mouth covering hers. Since he no longer had to support her weight, he was able to stroke her satiny skin with luxurious freedom.

The delicious sequence started all over again, even more fulfilling and tumultuous than before.

Brett was wakened a couple of hours after falling asleep by Sam grunting, then cursing under his breath.

"What's wrong?" she asked groggily.

"Damned if I know." He reached for the bedside light. "What in hell is that?"

She had to squint against the light, but she managed to see the object that had disturbed Sam.

"It's only Ashley."

Sam glared at the bassett hound. "This is carrying things too far. I refuse to share you with Ashley Wilkes."

Hiding a grin, Brett slipped out of bed, shivering at the cool night air. She lifted Ashley off the bed, set him on the floor, and walked to the door.

"Come on, Ashley. You never were respected for your delicate sensibilities."

Ashley finally made it out of the bedroom. Brett shut the door after him and, rubbing her arms, hurried back to the warm bed.

Sam had rolled on to his side and was leaning on his elbow, watching every move she made. "You arc a beautiful woman, Red."

She blinked, surprised by the serious tone of his voice. "I'm glad you think so."

He grasped one of her hands and tugged her down to lie beside him. "Ashley can creep back into your bed when I'm gone. Until then," he murmured as he pushed her onto her back, "I don't plan on sharing you with him or anyone else."

He kissed her with a possessive hunger, and Brett lost the chance to ask him how much time they had left. She wrapped her arms around his shoulders and gave herself over to the need to be as close to him as possible.

Some time later Brett opened her eyes and stared into the darkness of her bedroom. She had no idea what had wakened her this time from the dreamless sleep of exhaustion, or what time it was other than the sun hadn't come up yet. One of Sam's arms was under her, the other over her, with his long length pressed against her back, his head sharing her pillow. Even asleep, his strength, physical and emotional, made her feel secure and safe.

So why was she suddenly edgy, as though she were being threatened by some nebulous thing she couldn't name or recognize?

Awake himself, Sam felt the change in her breathing. "Can't sleep, Red?"

"I feel as though I've forgotten something vitally important, and I can't think of what it could be."

"It's understandable if you're a little keyed up. It isn't every day you have a fire in your barn."

She sighed. "That somebody started intentionally."

Sam turned her to face him as easily as if he were rearranging thistledown. Blinking several times, Brett propped herself up on one elbow and looked down at him. "There are definite disadvantages in being smaller than you."

"I wouldn't call them disadvantages," he murmured with amusement. "I doubt if we could have managed that episode against the bedroom door earlier if you were as big as I am."

"You just flipped me over like I was a stuffed teddy bear."

He chuckled. "The last thing you remind me of is a teddy bear. I simply like talking to your front better than I like talking to your back." When he saw her expression change, he asked, "What's wrong?"

"I just remembered what's been bothering me."

She flung back the covers and bounced over to the edge of the bed. The night had grown even colder, and she grabbed his shirt after turning on the bedside light.

"Modesty at this stage of our relationship?" he asked.

"Hypothermia," she replied. "It's cold in here."

After slipping on his shirt, she walked over to the door, where her jeans still lay on the floor.

"You don't plan on getting dressed right now, do you?" Sam asked as she picked the jeans up. "It's still the middle of the night."

She shook her head. "I put something in my pocket that I found in the barn. What with the questions from the police and the other stuff, I forgot all about it."

"Other stuff?" A corner of his mouth lifted slightly. "Couldn't you come up with a better description than that for our lovemaking?"

"I'll work on it." She shoved her hand into the front pocket of the jeans. "Aha!" Her fingers closed around a scrap of fabric. Withdrawing it from the pocket, she held it out to Sam. "Look at this!"

She had Sam's attention for a couple of reasons. One, she hadn't bothered to button his shirt when she'd put it on, and he kept catching tantalizing glimpses of her white breasts and dusky nipples. And two, his damn curiosity made it impossible for him to ignore what she was so excited about.

She sat on the edge of the bed near his hip and held out the scrap of material so he could see it.

"This was caught on a nail on the ladder to the loft. Unless I'm mistaken, it's from a man's suit. Since you and Hank and just about everyone else, except for the reenactors, were wearing casual clothes, my guess is this belongs to a well-dressed arsonist."

NINE

Early in the morning after the fire, Sam stood by the kitchen sink waiting for the electric coffeepot to finish perking. Even though he hadn't had much sleep, his mind had refused to shut down after Brett had showed him what she had found on the ladder. The torn material wasn't much of a clue, but other than the traces of kerosene found on some of the straw that hadn't burned, it was the only one they had. He'd finally given up on sleep and had come downstairs to think about everything that had happened during the night. Brett was awake, too, and would join him after she took a shower. Until then, he had the kitchen to himself. It would be another hour before Mrs. Arthur would be slamming pots and pans around.

He took the piece of gray material out of his pocket and examined it again. The scrap was about an inch by an inch and a half with charcoal threads running through several shades of gray. Sam stroked the fabric between his finger and thumb. He couldn't recall the name of the type of material, but he knew quality fabric when he felt it. The clean condition of the scrap also told him it hadn't been stuck on the ladder long. He couldn't see any hint of dust or discoloration that would indicate its owner had climbed the ladder some time ago.

When he'd first glimpsed the gray fabric, he had immediately thought of the Confederate uniforms the reenactors wore. On closer examination, he'd realized the material wasn't wool but a blend of wool and silk often found in expensive suits.

That deduction eliminated the reenactors. Even if he could have come up with a motive, he knew that none of the men and women affiliated with the regiments wore clothing made of that type of modern material.

His crew generally wore casual, serviceable clothing on location, except for the actors when they were in costume. He would check with wardrobe, but he was positive none of the costumes were made from fabric like this one.

Approaching the problem from a different slant, Sam considered motive alone. He couldn't think of a single reason why anyone would want to ruin the equipment stored in the barn or the building itself. Like Brett, his company was financially secure. Moreover, although Darren had arranged for more than adequate insurance to cover any eventuality, delaying production would hinder completion of the film, which in the long run would cost them more money. They had no valid reason to want production halted or even delayed by setting a fire in the barn.

The only reason for the fire that he could come up with was that someone wanted to discourage them from making the film. Since no one had been in the barn except the arsonist, a personal vendetta had to be ruled out. Unless someone wanted to harm something that belonged to Brett. But that didn't make any sense, since she hadn't done anything that would tick somebody off. She hadn't left Judson Quill's office on good terms, but Sam had trouble picturing the attorney lugging bales of straw and a can of kerosene up to the loft.

But the day Sam had met Quill, the pompous lawyer had been wearing a suit made of fabric similar to the scrap of material Brett had found.

Brett's search for her mother's journal, which could possibly name someone who might have been responsible for Melanie Southern's death, could worry that person. But no one except him knew what she was looking for in the house.

Sam poured himself some coffee and had lifted the mug to his mouth when Darren spoke behind him. "Would you pour me a cup too?"

Sam took down another thick mug out of the cupboard and poured coffee into it. Turning around, he handed it to Darren.

"Couldn't sleep either?" he asked.

Darren took the mug and walked over to the

table, sitting down heavily on one of the chairs. "There's nothing like a three-alarm fire to chase away any hope of getting to sleep." After taking a sip of the scalding coffee, Darren leaned back on two legs of the chair and looked at Sam. "Any ideas about what's going on?"

"A couple, but nothing definite."

"Anything you wish to share?"

Sam shook his head slowly. He didn't like keeping things from his partner, but the situation involving Brett's mother wasn't his to tell. Brett hadn't said not to say anything to Darren or anyone else, but she hadn't told him to spread it around either.

For his part, Darren hadn't said anything to Sam about his involvement with Brett. It had always been Sam's policy not to become involved with any of his actresses or female crew members. In fact, he didn't get involved with women at all during filming so he could concentrate fully on the job at hand. Until he met Brett, he hadn't had any difficulties keeping that self-imposed rule.

But he had met her, and he was sleeping with her. Maybe he wasn't being smart or practical, but he was being honest with himself. And he hoped, with Brett. He couldn't stay away from her.

Darren cleared his throat, the sound jarring Sam out of his reverie. "What's going on, Sam?"

Sam's mouth twisted into a mocking smile. "About a hundred different things. When I get them sorted out, I'll be in a better position to explain them to you."

"This one's different from the others, isn't she?"

"Brett?"

"No, idiot. The housekeeper. Of course I mean Brett."

The kitchen door was pushed open, and Brett entered. "Did I hear my name just now?"

"Yes, you did," Darren said, grinning at her as she rubbed her eyes. "We were talking about you behind your back. Now we can talk in front of you."

She waved one hand. "Go ahead. Don't mind me. I'll be the one seated at the end of the table drinking coffee."

Sam smiled at Darren. "Brett and I understand each other, Darren. There isn't anything we can do about the rumors floating around, but we're trying to be halfway discreet."

Darren nodded. "I agreed not to mention Brett's family in the publicity, and I haven't, even though she would make great copy."

Brett frowned at him. "Great copy?"

"Oh yeah," Darren said. "Beautiful southern woman living on a plantation that's been in the family since it was built. Mother died mysteriously. Father is off excavating Mayan ruins. Woman gave up career in the Big Apple to sweeten up a small town."

"Brett has to live here long after the documentary is finished," Sam said. "I promised we'd respect her privacy."

"I said she'd make great copy. I didn't say I was going to use it."

"Good. Let's drop the subject."

"That's fine with me," Darren said as he looked warily from Sam to Brett. "I don't enjoy having Chief Thunderhorn glowering at me from one side and Miss Southern Peach shooting daggers at me from the other."

Sam smiled. "I bet I can guess what you do enjoy."

"No contest. I enjoy making money. Which reminds me, if you're still interested in that book about the eighteenth-century glassblower, I need to pick up the option. Since we're on schedule and will be through here in a week, I want to get research cracking on the background. I'm going to send Elaine and Vernon to Boston on Monday or Tuesday and we'll follow as soon as we're done here."

Brett carefully set her mug down. Next week, she repeated silently. Sam would be gone next week.

Sam refilled her mug and Darren's, then his own. "Let's drop the subject for now. Do you have a copy of today's shooting schedule on you? I'm thinking of changing the sequence of scenes prior to the Union charge on the stone wall."

Brett's chest felt tight and painful until she realized she had been holding her breath ever since

Darren had said they would be leaving next week. Forcing herself to breathe, she pushed back her chair and excused herself. "I'll leave you two to discuss business and take off to tend to mine."

Sam looked up from the papers Darren had given him. Brett tilted her chin back and faced him. For a few moments they stared into each other's eyes, then Darren cleared his throat.

As though coming out of a trance, Brett shook her head and left the kitchen.

Her red coat and purse were by the back door. She grabbed them, finding her car keys in her purse. Her fingers closed around them, holding them so tightly, the uneven edges bit painfully into her palm.

She let herself out the back door and walked to her car. Morning dew had collected on the windshield, and she removed the excess with several swipes of her hand.

Inside the car, she turned on the wipers for a few seconds until the windshield was clear enough for her to see where she was going. She started the engine and backed out of the parking space. Gravel sprayed several feet behind her car when she pressed her foot down on the accelerator after changing gears. Her hands were sure and steady on the wheel as she drove away from the mansion and Sam. She had no idea where she was going. Her priority was just to get away from Maddox Hill. It didn't matter where.

Without making a conscious decision, she

ended up at Abbie Nelson's. Habit had her honking her horn in the prearranged signal she always used to let Abbie know who had arrived. She glanced at the clock on the dashboard of her car. Six in the morning was a hell of a time to come calling, even on close friends.

She was about to put the car in reverse and leave when the front door opened. Elsa stood in the open doorway and gestured for Brett to come in.

Brett shoved aside her misery when she saw the exhaustion around Elsa's eyes and the weary slump of her shoulders. Pushing open her car door, she got out and walked toward the house.

As she approached the bottom step, she asked, "Did Abbie have a bad night?"

Elsa shook her head. "An emergency call."

"I hope it wasn't anything serious."

"A new set of parents needed some reassurance. Their baby is fine. They're a wreck. I got home about ten minutes ago and just made a pot of coffee." She stepped back to make room for Brett to enter the house. As Brett passed her Elsa looked closely at her. "What's the matter?"

"How much time do you have?"

"However long it takes." Elsa shut the door and put her arm around Brett's waist as they walked together toward the kitchen. "Momma is up early, as usual. She heard your signal and probably has a cup of coffee poured for you already."

Entering the kitchen, Brett saw Abbie's sweet

welcoming smile and felt her throat tighten painfully. She walked up to Abbie's chair and knelt beside it, putting her arms around the older woman. She buried her face against Abbie's shoulder and closed her eyes. Abbie held her securely with one arm while her other hand stroked Brett's hair.

Neither woman rushed her or tried to soothe her with trite sayings and kind words. The only movement in the room was Abbie's fingers in Brett's hair and the sideways motion of the eyes and tail of a plastic black-cat wall clock.

Lifting her head, Brett smiled thinly. "I'm back to being twelve again," she said with wry humor, "and Johnny Spazac has just told me he's going to take Mary Lou Spencer to the May Day Dance instead of me. If I remember correctly, I ended up in the same position I am now."

Abbie's hand slid along Brett's cheek. "Feelings can get hurt at any age, child. Has Sam Horne hurt yours this time?"

Brett squeezed Abbie's hand before releasing it. She pulled out the chair between the two women and sat down at the table, calmed and comforted by the love of her friends. As Elsa had predicted, her mother had poured a cup of coffee for Brett, and it was sitting in front of her.

"I realized as I was driving here that Sam isn't at fault. I did this to myself."

She related the conversation between Darren and Sam. Then she described the events of the previous evening, including the fire, the police, and the bit of fabric she'd found on the ladder.

Both women listened quietly until Brett finished. Elsa was the first to speak. "Why would someone purposely set fire to your barn, Brett?"

"The obvious answer is that someone doesn't want the production company at Maddox Hill."

"Well, whoever did it either isn't very good at arson or didn't really want to burn down the entire building. You said the amount of kerosene used hadn't been enough to do much damage."

"That's what the firemen reported. They also pointed out that whoever started the fire knew there wasn't any straw in the loft. He brought his own, but the straw was damp and didn't burn very well."

"The guy is either dumb or made all those mistakes intentionally," Elsa said. "Is it possible someone simply wanted to get your attention, to warn you?"

"About what? I own a specialty gift shop, hardly a threat to anyone."

Abbie's quiet voice intervened. "Are you still searching for answers about your mother's death?"

Brett stared at the woman. She shouldn't be amazed at Abbie's perceptiveness after all this time, but in this case, she was. Somehow the blind woman saw things that the sighted couldn't see, even when it was right in front of their faces.

"How did you know?"

"I've heard your voice when you've occasionally asked me about Melanie. Did I know if she was upset about anything? Had she complained about not feeling well shortly before she died? Had she said anything about any problems between her and your father? You weren't satisfied with the verdict the authorities came up with of your mother's death, so I wondered if you had been actively investigating whatever theories you might have."

"You don't believe she took her own life either, Abbie. You knew my mother better than anyone. You know she wouldn't have taken even one sleeping pill. She certainly wouldn't have swallowed the amount the medical examiner found in her system. Someone had put the medication in her tea. The police found an empty pot and cup on her bedside table."

"Both of which had been washed," Elsa added. "I thought that was odd."

"Or some other method was used without her being suspicious," Brett went on. "Then when she became sleepy, someone guided her toward the stairs and pushed her down them so it would appear she fell after ingesting sleeping pills."

"Who would hate your mother that much, they'd go to such extremes to kill her?" Elsa asked.

"As far as I know, she didn't have an enemy in the world. For someone to arrange to have sleeping pills with them when they came to Maddox Hill means premeditation. It wasn't a spur-of-the-moment thing. My father knew of nothing that would cause someone to want to kill her." Brett looked at

Abbie. "I was completely stumped as to how I was going to prove my suspicions until I realized her journal for this year is missing. I'm hoping there will be some entry, some notation that will give me a clue as to who could have killed her."

Abbie tapped her fingers absently on the table as she thought over what Brett had said. Then she asked, "Where have you looked?"

Brett described her search of the rooms on the upper floors of the mansion, her father's office, the kitchen, the library, all the places where her mother might have kept the journal. All of the secret passages had been examined, even though her mother never cared to enter any of them because she didn't like confined places.

"I haven't checked the parlor, the conservatory, or the dining room yet, although I don't hold much hope for finding her journal in any of those rooms. I even went through her greenhouse, but I didn't find anything that would help."

"What about her treasure box?" the older woman asked.

Brett stared at Abbie. She vaguely remembered a wooden box with a brass clasp that she had seen when she was small. At one time it had been a display case that held a hundred cigars. Her mother had told her the box had been given to her by an uncle who said only valuable treasures should be kept inside it. Her mother had raised the lid with reverence and carefully taken out each item, as though they were made of precious stones. Brett remembered a ribbon, a seashell, an acorn with a face drawn on it, a small purple bottle of Blue Danube perfume, a stone with a fossilized leaf in it, among other childhood memorabilia. Shortly afterward, her mother had given Brett a small wooden chest of her own to use for her treasures.

"I haven't thought about that box for years." Brett frowned. "I don't remember seeing it among her belongings. I wonder where it could be."

Abbie pushed her chair back and stood. With one hand outstretched in front of her, the older woman left the kitchen. Elsa and Brett looked at each other with similar puzzled expressions on their faces. They could hear a drawer being opened and closed, then the sound of Abbie's felt slippers on the polished wooden floor in the hallway. When she reentered the kitchen, she had the wooden cigar box in her hand.

She carefully placed it on the table near Brett. "Your mother brought this over a day or so before the electricians were scheduled to update the wiring in the mansion. I believe it was about a week before she died. I thought it was odd at the time, considering that she had many more valuable things at Maddox Hill she didn't appear concerned about. Then she died. As you know, I was still adjusting to being blind then." Abbie paused for a few moments to compose herself. "I didn't think of this box until you mentioned her journal. Her journals, as I remember, were usually about five inches by seven. One would fit her treasure box if she still used that size."

Brett stared at the box. Apprehension tingled up and down her spine, like slivers of ice. The answers she was looking for could be in her mother's treasure box, or the contents could be the same as they'd been when Brett was a child. Either way, opening the box was going to affect her search for answers. This was basically her last chance, and she was hesitant about taking it. If the answer was in the box, her life would undergo a drastic change. If there was no clue at all, she would have to wonder until she died what really happened to her mother. The box and its contents were her last hope, and she found hope very difficult to give up.

Elsa placed her hand on Brett's arm. "One of my patients was recently diagnosed with leukemia, and when I told his mother, she said a curious thing. She naturally had wanted to know what was wrong with her child and now that she knew, she said, she had an enemy she could fight, an enemy with a name. If you find the journal in this box and your mother wrote something in it that implicates someone in her death, your enemy will have a name. Not knowing that name might be safer than knowing."

Brett met her friend's gaze. "I have to know one way or the other. For myself, for my father, and especially for my mother." She turned to Abbie. "Abbie, do you understand why I have to know for sure what happened to her?"

"Of course, child," the older woman said gently. "If someone took Melanie's life, that person cannot get away with ending her existence before it was her time."

Brett rubbed her suddenly damp hands on the thighs of her slacks. Taking a deep breath, she snapped open the clasp and lifted the lid.

Elsa leaned forward to see inside. "Well?" Abbie asked. "Is the journal there?"

"Yes," Brett murmured. "It's here."

When Abbie didn't hear movement, she prodded: "Are you going to read the entries? If so, please read them aloud."

The pleasant scent of dried herbs rose from the box as Brett reached in to remove the journal. She set it on the table in front of her, opened it to the middle, and read aloud instructions for planting garlic.

The three women smiled at the earnest wording of the directions, written as exacting and painstakingly detailed as a formula for an important medical discovery. Melanie had always taken her research very seriously, and it showed in her writing.

Brett leafed through several more pages, reading bits and pieces of planting schedules, descriptions of what had been picked to be dried, and how the hand cream she'd made had helped Mrs. Arthur's dry skin.

Disappointed, Brett turned a couple more pages. "At least now I can stop looking for her journal." Flipping over another page, she glanced at a few lines, then looked closer. "Oh, my God," she breathed.

Abbie and Elsa said in tandem, "What!"

Brett silently read through the paragraph that had caught her attention, then she read it aloud.

" 'Judson asked me not to tell Phillip about his situation. I tried to persuade Judson to go to Dr. Chambers when he said the chamomile tea concoction had no effect. I mentioned that Dr. Chambers is a qualified psychologist, and Judson became quite agitated, and I'm concerned he will do something rash.' "

No one spoke for a long time after Brett finished reading. Finally Abbie said quietly, "I don't believe Judson Quill would do anything to cause your mother any pain. He adored her. He has ever since they were children."

"I find it hard to believe too," Elsa said. "Judson Quill has always impressed me as being full of hot air at times, but collapses like a pricked balloon if someone stands up to him."

Brett didn't take her gaze away from the journal. She turned page after page, reading excerpts when something caught her eye. After going back a number of pages, then forward to the last entry, she didn't find any other references to the lawyer or his problems. She did see Kathryn's name several times with herb plants listed after it. Melanie had probably given those plants to Kathryn.

"Listen," she said, then read, " 'As hardy as the mint and rosemary are, I feel they will not survive Kathryn's smothering attention. Her reason for wanting the plants was simply stated as being necessary because Judson said I know so much about herbs. Kathryn wants Judson to think she is as smart as I am. Such a sad woman.' "

Elsa got up to fetch the coffeepot. Refilling their cups, she said, "It certainly sounds like Judson has his hands full with his second wife. Chamomile is used as a calming agent for nerves and stress. It's possible Judson asked for herbal remedies for Kathryn."

"What if," Brett said thoughtfully, "I call Judson and ask him to meet me somewhere? Not at the office where he could pull rank as my attorney. Somewhere else where he would feel more inclined to talk. I talked to other friends of mother's after she died, hoping to find some clue as to what really happened. I never discussed her with Judson, though."

Abbie sat back in her chair and turned her head toward Brett. "Judson was too distraught after Melanie died to have been much help. If you do meet him, you need to have a safety net in case Judson is not as rational as we think he is, someone who could come to your rescue if the situation gets out of hand. A blind woman and her reed-thin daughter are not going to be much help."

Brett knew what Abbie was going to say next. "I

can handle this on my own, Abbie. I'll be expecting trouble and my mother wasn't. The outcome will be completely different."

As though Brett hadn't said a word, Abbie continued, "What you need is Sam Horne."

TEN

Sam tried extremely hard to concentrate on the shooting schedule that day. In the morning they rehearsed the Union charge on the stone wall near the Sunken Road, the most dramatic scene in the documentary. Throughout the afternoon, they filmed the attack in numerous takes from various angles, until Sam was certain he had enough to work with. Now they were getting ready for one last shot before the sun set.

Sam's thoughts, however, kept shifting to earlier that morning, when he had called Brett's shop and she hadn't answered. Her assistant Myra had. Discovering Brett wasn't at Southern Touch had bothered him. Myra had told him that Brett had called to say she wouldn't be in until late that afternoon.

It wasn't like her to change her plans without telling him. She had told him before her shower that she had a lot to do at the store that day, and she was counting on Myra to help with customers and filling orders while she went over her books.

He and Brett had settled into a routine of sorts in the short time he'd been staying at Maddox Hill. Each morning as they dressed they told each other what the day had in store for them. It was a quiet, intimate time, ordinary to some people perhaps, but special to Sam, for he'd never experienced anything like it.

In the brief time he'd known her, he'd learned that even the smallest common activity became magical with Brett.

Instead of looking through the viewfinder at the layout in front of him as he was supposed to be doing, Sam stared off into space and thought about the rush of warmth that had flooded his chest when he had watched Brett brush her teeth yesterday morning. Brush her teeth, for crying out loud. Such a simple thing, and he had been overwhelmed with a strange combination of emotions; a blending of affection, arousal, and contentment.

Hank coughed a couple of times. "Ah, Sam. You wanted to check the angle."

Sam went through the motions of looking through the viewfinder. The fading sunlight was coming through the trees on Marye Heights, creating a picturesque sight in sharp contrast to the shocking scene of hundreds of Union soldiers lying on the grass incline leading up to the formidable stone wall. Actually, the death total had been nine thousand, but Sam had compensated for the numbers by shooting groupings of bodies to make the hundreds of reenactors appear to be many more.

Smoke drifted across the top of the gray stone wall where Confederate soldiers had stood four deep to steadily bombard the attacking army. The setting sun added just the right touch of pathos to the bloody aftermath of the battle.

"It's exactly what I wanted, Hank. Let's get it the first time before the sun disappears."

Stepping back to let Hank do his job, Sam tried to ignore the chill of dread that had been steadily enveloping him since that morning.

His usual concentration was being blown to bits by an auburn-haired chocolatier who seemed to have disappeared off the face of the earth. Or at least from this small corner of the universe.

Where in the hell was she? he wondered, for the thousandth time.

The important scene was completed to his satisfaction, and he instructed Hank to take a few more feet of film of the overall layout just in case more was needed when they edited.

Darren called out to him and Sam looked around, finding his partner holding out a cellular telephone. His long strides ate up the ground as he quickly walked over to Darren.

"Is it Brett?"

Darren shook his head. "Some woman named Nelson. Terry said she's been calling all over for you. Says it's important she talk to you."

"Nelson? I don't know any—" Sam suddenly realized who it was and grabbed the phone. "Abbie? This is Sam Horne. Do you happen to know where Brett is?"

The older woman's voice was so soft, Sam had to strain to hear her. The chatter of the crew wasn't helping either. Holding his hand over the phone, he yelled, "Quiet!" He was instantly obeyed, a stillness falling over the crew and the reenactors, some of whom stopped being dead and sat up.

Removing his hand, Sam spoke into the phone. "I'm sorry, Abbie, but I couldn't hear you. Would you repeat what you said?"

He listened intently to every word Brett's friend said, his jaw tightening, his eyes narrowing, his knuckles turning white with the force of his grip on the receiver.

Darren and Terry exchanged glances, their expressions showing a mixture of curiosity and concern. They had both witnessed the rare occasion when Sam lost his temper and the signs were obvious that a bout of anger was imminent.

The gentle tone of Sam's voice was in direct opposition to his stony expression as he finally asked, "What time is this meeting supposed to take place?"

As he listened to Abbie's answer he glanced at his watch. He had exactly twenty minutes to get from the Sunken Road to Old Town Fredericksburg.

"Try not to worry, Abbie. I'll see that nothing happens to Brett." He didn't tell the older woman that Brett was in more danger from him for what she was planning to do than from the idiotic meeting she had arranged.

He disconnected the call and quickly punched out the phone number for Southern Touch. The lines around his mouth stretched even tighter as he listened to the phone ring without anyone answering it.

He tossed the phone to Terry and, grabbing her pen, wrote a number on the back of her hand. "Keep calling that number until someone answers. If it's Brett, tell her I'm on my way. If a man comes on the line, hang up and phone the police and tell them to go to Southern Touch Gift Shop."

As he passed Darren he took the other man's arm and pulled him along with him. "Now's your chance to show me how you got that speeding ticket in Fresno. Where'd you park your car?"

"Next to the visitors' center. Why?" Darren nearly fell over a curb that came up faster than he expected. "Dammit, Sam. What the hell is going on?"

"I'm going to strangle a southern woman with my own two hands," he said tightly, quickening his step when he spotted Darren's red rental car. "Then I'm going to tell her she's going to marry me and stop tormenting me."

Using what little breath he had left from the mad dash to his car, Darren chuckled as he settled behind the wheel and shoved the key into the ignition. "I thought the tormenting started after the marriage ceremony."

"Brett Southern doesn't do anything like anyone else. Like tell a man who cares about her that she's setting herself up as bait so he could be there to protect her."

"What in hell are you talking about?"

Looking at the road ahead, Sam said, "Drive faster, and I'll tell you."

Brett heard a noise and squeezed the decorator bag too hard. It couldn't be the phone. She'd unplugged it so she wouldn't have to worry about answering it. Taking a deep breath to calm herself, she realized the sound was only the compressor on the refrigerator doing its usual shuddering. That mystery solved, she looked down at the mold she was working on. A large blob of pink chocolate had fallen onto it. She picked up a narrow spatula and scraped off the excess candy, her mouth twisting in chagrin when she saw how the spatula was shaking.

Great, she thought. Her stomach was in knots, her fingers were trembling, and her hands were sweating. This had seemed like such a good idea when she'd first thought of it. Even after she'd called Judson and asked him to meet her at her store after closing time, she had still considered her plan a good one. Now she wasn't sure.

Gritting her teeth, she continued pretending to

work as usual, the general idea being that she wasn't too concerned about her meeting with Judson. Actually, she was a nervous wreck.

When she heard the gentle clang of the bell above the door, the butterflies in her stomach became starving vultures.

She regretted the idea of pretending to be casually working while she chatted with Judson, who might not be as close a friend to Melanie as everyone thought. Jealousy came in many forms and in a variety of ways. Brett was having difficulty imagining Judson with strong feelings for anyone or anything, but perhaps it was true that still waters did run deep.

She nearly dropped the decorator bag when Judson suddenly walked into the back room. Dressed as usual in a three-piece suit, he looked exactly as she'd always seen him: professional, somber, and solid.

"This is most unusual, Brett," he said with a touch of censure in his tone. "I would have thought your accountant would have been the appropriate person to call if you want advice about your business."

"I didn't ask you here to talk business, Judson."

"You said you had something to show me and that I was to meet you at your shop at five-thirty. I took it for granted you needed my advice about some business decision."

Brett gave up any pretense of making candy. Setting the bag down, she turned to face him squarely. "It seems we've both been taking things for granted. Take me, for example. I took it for granted that you and your wife were my parents' best friends, that you would never do anything to hurt either one of them, or me, for that matter."

"And you would be quite correct." He didn't bother to conceal his impatience. "I wish you would get to the point, Brett. Kathryn isn't feeling well, and I should be with her."

Her mother's journal was lying on the worktable. She reached over to pick it up.

"Do you know what this is?"

"No, I don't," he said with a martyred sigh. "Is that what you wanted to show me?"

"I don't know if you are aware that my mother kept a journal in which she recorded herbal remedies, experiments with planting new herbs, and recipes she'd found in books or been given by other herbalists."

"I'm sure it is quite fascinating to someone interested in that sort of thing, but I still don't understand why you wanted me to come here this evening."

Brett wondered if it was her imagination that he seemed to be more guarded in his speech. "After my mother died, I couldn't believe she killed herself or fell down the stairs accidentally."

It could have been the lighting in the workroom, but Judson appeared to be paler than he'd been when he'd arrived. He glanced at the journal in her hand. "Evidently you feel you have found the answers you wanted."

Brett opened the journal to the page she had marked with a slip of paper. Without any warning, she read the passage her mother had written about Judson two days before her death. When she looked up, she saw Judson reach out to grab the edge of the worktable. Brett took a step toward him, fearing he was about to faint. His eyes were dark and anguished in a chalky white face.

"I didn't realize your mother kept a record of personal, confidential discussions."

"She usually didn't. She was obviously upset about whatever problem you had that you didn't want her to discuss with my father."

"Brett, you surely don't think I was involved with your mother in any way other than as her friend?"

"I don't know what to think." Brett walked to the sink to fill a paper cup with water for Judson. With her attention solely on him, she didn't hear the opening and closing of the door to the shop.

"Would you like to sit down?" she asked as she held out the paper cup to him.

He shook his head. He did accept the cup, however.

"Judson, I need to know what really happened the night my mother died."

After taking a long drink, he met her eyes. "I wouldn't ever do anything to hurt Melanie in any way. I cared about her and your father a great deal."

"You loved her, Jud," a sneering voice said from the doorway. "And not like a friend. Why deny it when we both know it's true?"

Brett jerked her head around to stare at the woman who had spoken. Kathryn Quill, like her husband, was dressed in a suit, hers almost a carbon copy of his. Her usually immaculate hairstyle was untidy, however, as though she had yanked at the sides of her head.

It was the look in the other woman's eyes that held Brett's attention. The socially correct bland expression was gone, replaced by a dark glare of hatred.

Brett's gaze dropped to the object Kathryn held in her hand. The barrel of the small handgun was pointed at her!

Judson took a step toward his wife. "Kathryn, put down the gun. You don't want to hurt Brett. She's done nothing to harm you. Give me the gun before you do something foolish."

The gun never wavered as Kathryn looked at Judson. "She's Melanie's daughter." Venom dripped from the woman's voice. "Melanie the good. Melanie the perfect. Just like your first wife, Jud. Even after fifteen years of marriage, I still have to listen to people talk about the saintly Ellen O'Hara Quill. What a wonderful woman she was, so charitable to those less fortunate than she, so generous with her time, which she gave freely to anyone in need."

Judson held out his hand toward his wife. "Give me the gun, Kathryn. Then we'll sit down and talk."

Kathryn shook her head. Her pink-tinted mouth twisted in a grimace of distaste. "Talking is your answer to everything, Jud. I prefer action. If something or someone is in my way, I get rid of them quickly. I don't talk them to death."

Brett forgot about the gun as she sorted out the pieces of the puzzle she'd connected incorrectly. "The chamomile tea was for you, not Judson, wasn't it, Kathryn? You were the one my mother was trying to help."

"Your dear mother was working with Jud to keep me doped up so Jud could sneak away to be with her."

Judson shook his head vehemently. "I have told you at least a hundred times that Melanie and Phillip were our dearest friends, and that is all they were."

"When you say *our*, you mean yours and Ellen's, don't you? Your friends were never *my* friends. They put up with me because they felt sorry for you, married to me. No matter what I did, it was never enough to gain Melanie's respect. Even the night I saw her for the last time, she looked at me as though I was something that had crawled in under the door."

Brett closed her eyes and counted to ten in an

attempt to control her fury. This unbalanced, vain woman had killed her mother.

After reaching ten, Brett opened her eyes and saw Kathryn raise the gun as Judson took another step toward her. "Don't try any heroics, Jud. Actually, I did Miss Southern a favor."

Brett stared at her in astonishment. "By killing my mother?"

"You and I have a lot in common, you know. Like Jud's first wife, your mother would be a hard act for you to follow through life. You would always have people comparing you to her, and you would always come up short in their eyes. Now you're free of her shadow."

"If you expect me to thank you for killing my mother, you're crazier than I thought."

Out in the front room, Sam curled his hands into fists as he heard Brett antagonizing a woman who was holding a gun. Darren was crouched beside him, ready to spring through the doorway at Sam's signal. It was Darren who had seen the shadowy figure of a woman through the glass in the front door. He had then pointed to the bell hanging near the top of the door. Being taller than Sam, he had slipped his hand through the barely opened door to hold the bell's clapper so they could enter the store without making any noise.

Sam's first impulse had been to charge the woman, but then he'd seen the gun pointed at Brett. He couldn't take the chance Kathryn Quill would pull the trigger if he and Darren jumped her from behind. They would have to wait for just the right moment. In the meantime he felt fear clutching his gut with sharp claws at the thought of anything happening to Brett.

Brett, on the other hand, seemed fearless as she continued to goad the other woman. "How did you do it, Kathryn? How did you kill my mother?"

"I wish you wouldn't keep saying that," Kathryn said petulantly. "I didn't so much kill your mother as I removed my competition. I've found that works the best. Remember the car accident the chairwoman of the charity ball had two years ago when she broke her leg? Jud's first wife had once been the chairwoman, and your mother also. I was nominated, but Sylvia Armstead won the most votes. Then she had the nerve to appoint me as her assistant, as if I wouldn't notice what a slap in the face that was. So I arranged a little accident for dear Sylvia. At our next meeting, I slipped outside and put some petroleum jelly on the brake pedal of her car, enough to make it slippery. When she went around that curve at the bottom of the hill near her house, her foot slipped off the brake, and, just my luck, she rammed into the side of a truck. Broke her leg, and I got to be chairwoman."

Brett knew she should be horrified by Kathryn's matter-of-fact relating of an incident in which she had intentionally set out to hurt, or even kill, someone. But all Brett could feel was anger at the senseless acts of vanity.

"You are certifiable," she said quietly.

Kathryn's mouth tightened into a grim line. "You're wrong. A crazy person couldn't have come up with a foolproof scheme time and time again to get rid of competition without being caught. That takes someone with a clever mind, not someone who's lost it."

"How did you get my mother to take the sleeping pills?"

"I chose a night when your father was scheduled to give a lecture and would be gone for hours. I waited in the walk-in closet off her bedroom until she came upstairs. I knew she had the habit of bringing a pot of chamomile tea to her room each night to drink while she read some of her plant books. She practiced what she preached." She glanced at her husband and sneered. "Jud informed me of that as an incentive to persuade me to drink the horrible stuff."

"Then what did you do?" Brett asked to bring Kathryn's attention back to the night Melanie had died.

"While Melanie was in the bathroom, I slipped out of the closet and put a handful of ground-up sleeping pills into the pot of tea. I waited what seemed like forever, but when I finally came back out of the closet, she was still awake. When she saw me, she tried to get out of bed, but she was too woozy from the pills. I pretended to let her escort me to the door, but when we reached the top of the stairs, I gave her a little push and she toppled over."

The cavalier way Kathryn spoke of her mother's death infuriated Brett so much, she could barely keep from rushing at the woman. "My mother always went out of her way to make you feel welcome in our house," she said, her voice shaking with her fury, "and you show your appreciation by drugging her and pushing her down her own stairs. What kind of person could do such a thing?"

Kathryn raised her free hand to the side of her head and clenched her fingers in her hair. It was as though she had so much restless energy, she needed an outlet, even if she hurt herself in the process.

When she brought her arm down, her hand was shaking. She clasped both hands on the gun and kept it pointed at Brett.

"You've had everything handed to you, Miss Brett," Kathryn said with a sneer. "You don't know what it's like to want something, only to be turned down."

Brett thought she saw a shadow move just beyond the doorway, then was certain someone was in the front of the shop when she heard a table leg scrape on the wood floor.

Unfortunately, Kathryn heard the sound also. She turned and pointed the gun toward the dark shop.

Brett spoke again, hoping to bring Kathryn's attention back to her. If it was Sam in the front room, she certainly didn't want Kathryn to start shooting in that direction. As for herself, her anger and disgust were stronger than her fear, making her search for some sort of explanation for this woman's senseless violence.

"When you were told there was no part for you in the documentary Sam Horne is filming, did you decide there wouldn't be a documentary at all if you couldn't be in it?"

Kathryn's grip on the gun wavered, but it was once again aimed in Brett's direction.

"I saw a program on television," she said, "where a fire in another room caused water damage when the firefighters put out the blaze. Isn't it a shame about Mr. Horne's movie? All that film soaked in water and foam."

"The film wasn't damaged, Mrs. Quill," Sam said from behind Kathryn. "We use watertight containers."

Kathryn swung around, the gun waving wildly, and Brett rushed at her. She grabbed Kathryn's right wrist hard and pushed her arm up just as the gun went off. The bullet lodged in the ceiling above their heads. Sam and Darren wrested the gun away from Kathryn, then Sam clamped her arms behind her back.

"Brett," he said. "Find something to keep Mrs. Quill from doing anything even more dumb than she's already managed to do."

As Darren called the police Brett found a roll of the heavy packing tape she used to close boxes. Kathryn struggled and cursed as they wound the tape around her wrists, securing her hands behind her back. The two of them together were physically stronger than Kathryn, but she had the strength that came from madness. Even after they'd finished with the tape, Sam had his hands full keeping Kathryn restrained so she wouldn't hurt herself, him, or anyone else.

Judson, Brett noticed, hadn't moved since Kathryn had first admitted to killing Melanie. He stood several feet away from his wife, his gaze never leaving her. His shoulders were slumped in defeat, his eyes haunted with the knowledge of what his wife had done. And what he'd allowed her to do.

As pathetic as the older man looked, Brett couldn't feel any sympathy for him. He hadn't actually killed her mother, but his culpability stemmed from knowing his wife was mentally unstable and doing nothing about it. He *had* to have known, Brett thought. Kathryn's feelings of hate and jealousy hadn't developed overnight.

"I'm going to tell the police everything, Judson," she said to him. "You are just as guilty as Kathryn because you knew what she was doing and didn't stop her. You're an attorney, for God's sake. You're supposed to uphold the law, not break it."

The lawyer slowly turned his head toward her. With the air of a man completely defeated, he said quietly, "I can't ask you to forgive me when I can't find forgiveness for myself. I'm sorry for Melanie's death. I swear I didn't know what Kathryn had

done. I'm also sorry she set the fire in your barn."
He glared at Sam. "She became even more irra-
tional when she couldn't get a part in your film.
She was sure people would accept her if she had an
important role."

"You knew your wife was ill," Sam said. "Why
didn't you do something about it?"

Judson's faint smile held a lifetime of sadness.
"A man will put up with a great deal for the woman
he loves."

"Up to a point," Sam said, looking at Brett.
"You don't let her get into situations where she's
going to get into trouble or hurt herself."

Before Brett could respond, they all heard a
police siren scream to a halt in front of the store.
Darren went to the doorway and beckoned the officers into the back room.

Brett succinctly told them the situation while
Kathryn raged at her, Sam, the policemen. Judson
confirmed what Brett said. The two policemen
couldn't hide their astonishment at hearing the
prominent Fredericksburg lawyer confess to being
an accomplice after the fact to murder. Although
Kathryn continued struggling, Judson went along
with the policemen willingly.

A feeling of anticlimax hung over the back
room after the officers left with the Quills. Brett
sighed and leaned against the worktable.

"I guess it's over," she said.

"Not quite," Sam said. He grabbed her hand

and started walking toward the door of the workroom. "Darren, I'm taking your car. Can you find your way back to Maddox Hill?"

"Sure. Where are you going?"

"To the battlefield. It seems appropriate."

ELEVEN

Driving Darren's rental car, Sam took Lee Drive, which stretched through the Fredericksburg battlefield. They passed a pair of energetic people pedaling their bicycles, and Sam kept driving until he came to an area where he could safely pull off the road without blocking it.

He shut off the engine. Brett remained where she was until Sam walked around the front of the car and opened her door.

She looked up at him. Puzzled by their destination, she said, "I've seen the battlefield."

He reached down and clasped her wrist. "Not with me."

That was true enough, she mused, but then there were a lot of things she hadn't done with him. Silly things like opening up Christmas presents together, or taking care of him when he had the flu, or seeing one of his documentaries with him.

Because he was stronger than she was and she didn't have the energy for a tug-of-war, she got out of the car. About ten feet away from them she could see a long grass-covered mound of raised earth, which was the overgrown remains of a trench dug during the war.

She needed more of a defense than a trench to hide in to ward off the pain that would come with the end of their affair, she thought wearily. She looked around at the nearby trees. The only sound was leaves brushing against one another over their heads.

"Leave it to a director to set up the scene with the right backdrop," she mused aloud. "Privacy for the showdown. No fragile objects that can be thrown and broken. A helluva walk back to town if I don't feel like hearing what you're about to say. The only thing missing is soft music in the background. Or do you have a trumpet player in the woods ready to play taps?"

Sam shook his head. "You're reading the wrong script, Red. This isn't a farewell scene."

"If you have seduction in mind, I had better remind you of the intrepid bikers we passed a few minutes ago. They might not be the romantic sort and might report us. The publicity wouldn't hurt you any, but I wouldn't care for it."

Sam leaned back against the trunk of a tree and watched her with that intensity she'd never quite gotten used to. "What do you care about?"

"I care that you're leaving soon and there's nothing I can do about it."

"Maybe there is."

"Before this morning and your little talk with Darren about flitting off to Boston, I might have thought so. I might have thought something silly, like we had something special between us that would make it impossible for either one of us to leave the other."

He didn't agree or disagree, which was really irritating.

When he continued to watch her without saying anything, Brett felt her bravado slipping away, leaving her defenseless and vulnerable. She wanted a clean break, executed quickly and efficiently, not drawn out painfully until she felt cut in two by a dull blade.

"Are you through?" he asked.

She nodded, afraid if she said anything, it would come out in a sob.

"Good." He pushed away from the tree and approached her. "Now it's my turn, so kindly be quiet until I'm finished." He cupped her face in his hands, forcing her to meet his gaze. "I don't want to leave you, Red. I'm afraid that if I do, I would end up crawling back on my hands and knees to beg you to take me back."

She wasn't sure what he was saying, but a glint of hope sparked through her sadness. "I knew going into this affair, Sam, that you would be leaving after your film was done." She swallowed back a little sob and added bravely, "I would like us to part friends at least, if that's possible."

He shook his head, and her hope died, her heart sank.

She dropped her gaze to the front of his shirt, unable to continue the charade of being a good sport.

When she heard him chuckle, she lifted her lashes and glared at him, making him laugh all the harder. "I'm glad I found out now about your sick sense of humor," she snapped. "How can you laugh at me when—" Her voice broke and she bit her lip.

"When what?" he asked softly. "Finish what you were going to say, Red."

Taking a deep breath, she said, "I don't think it's funny that I love you, and you won't even let us be friends when you leave."

Satisfaction flared in his eyes. His arms swept around her and he pulled her into his embrace. He buried his face in her throat and sighed heavily, as though he'd been on a long march and had finally made it home.

When he raised his head and met her gaze, Brett was astounded to see a hint of moisture in his doe-brown eyes.

"Sam?"

"We can't part friends because we can't part, Brett," he said simply. "When I have to leave, I want you to be with me. We'll have to talk about where we're going to live, whether you want to sell your business or I move the production company to the East Coast. We can discuss all of that stuff later after you've agreed to marry me."

"Marry you? Me? You? Marry?" She said the words as though they were foreign to her tongue. Not only did she have trouble saying them, she was having an even bigger difficulty understanding what they meant.

"Don't give me the song-and-dance about we haven't known each other very long," he said. "I knew when I saw you stomp across that street in Old Town carrying the baby basket that you were going to be trouble, and I was right. I found myself wanting to see you, to see your eyes snap when you argued with me. To touch you. Lord, I wanted to touch you," he said with feeling. "Couldn't you tell when we made love how much I needed you? I nearly went up in flames every time we came together. That should have given you a hint as to how you affected me."

Brett felt her cheeks grow warm with a blush. "I just thought you were good in bed."

He chuckled. "It takes two, Red. Are you going to answer my question or do you have to think about it?"

She frowned, puzzled. "What question?"

"About marrying me."

"You never asked me. You told me in the same sort of tone you would use if you suggested we have soup rather than salad. You've obviously never directed a romance. That's not the way it's done."

He inclined his head and studied her for a few seconds. "I'm never too old to learn. Perhaps if you gave me some idea of how it's done, I can improve my performance."

Brett heard the sound of tires on the road as the bikers came around the curve. She took Sam's hand and drew him between several trees. A canopy of leaves overhead shadowed the spot where they were standing. With the moon rising over the horizon, it seemed as though they were the only two people in the world once the bikers disappeared from sight.

Facing him, she touched his face with her hands. "The sun seems brighter, the air seems clearer, the whole world is happier when I'm with you. I could go on breathing, working, living if you weren't in my life, but I wouldn't find any joy in any of those things without you. I love your arrogance, your humor, your touch, your smile. I love you. I want to take your name as a sign I trust you with my heart for the rest of my life. I want to marry you."

Sam's voice sounded oddly strangled as he sighed her name and put his arms around her as though she was made of fine crystal. He covered her mouth with his and kissed her deeply for a very long time.

When he felt able to speak without making a fool of himself by blubbering, he touched her face as she had his and said, "I never understood how the Duke of Windsor could have given up his throne because of love until I met you. I was like those hidden passages in your house. You were the only one who knew how to unlock the secret recesses of my heart. Everything I thought was vital to my happiness is nothing compared to the joy I feel when you smile at me. I need you to marry me and live with me and love me for the rest of our lives."

Tears of happiness welled up in her eyes. "Okay," she said.

Sam laughed and lifted her up in his arms to twirl her around and around. The leaves rustled under his feet, and the wind blew the leaves on the branches over their heads.

But all they saw was each other and the glorious future spreading out in front of them.

YOU'VE READ THE BOOK.
NOW DOUBLE YOUR FUN BY ENTERING
LOVESWEPT'S TREASURED TALES III CONTEST!

Everybody loves a good romance, especially when that romance is inspired by a beloved fairy tale, legend, even a Shakespearean play. It's an entertaining challenge for the writer to create a contemporary retelling of a classic story—and for you, the reader, to find the similarities between the retold story and the classic.

For example:

- While reading STALKING THE GIANT by Victoria Leigh, did you notice that the heroine's nickname is exactly the same as the giant-slayer's in "Jack and the Beanstalk"?
- How about the fact that, like Adam and Eve, the hero and heroine in Glenna McReynold's DRAGON'S EDEN are alone in a paradise setting?
- Surely the heroine's red cape in HOT SOUTHERN NIGHTS by Patt Bucheister reminded you of the one Little Red Riding Hood wears on the way to her grandma's house.
- You couldn't have missed the heroine's rebuffing of the hero in Peggy Webb's CAN'T STOP LOVING YOU. Kate, in Shakespeare's *Taming of the Shrew*, displays the same steeliness when dealing with Petruchio.

The four TREASURED TALES III romances this month contain many, many more wonderful similarities to the classic stories they're based on. And with LOVESWEPT'S TREASURED TALES III CONTEST, you have a once-in-a-lifetime opportunity to let us know how many of these similarities you found. Even better, because this is LOVESWEPT's third year of publishing TREASURED TALES, this contest will have **three winners!**

Read the Official Rules to find out what you need to do to enter LOVESWEPT'S TREASURED TALES III CONTEST.

Now, indulge in the magic of TREASURED TALES III —and grab a chance to win some treasures of your own!

LOVESWEPT'S TREASURED TALES III CONTEST

OFFICIAL RULES:

1. *No purchase is necessary.* Enter by printing or typing your name, address, and telephone number at the top of one (or more, if necessary) piece(s) of 8½" X 11" plain white paper, if typed, or lined paper, if handwritten. Then list each of the similarities you found in one or more of the TREASURED TALES III romances to the classic story each is based on. The romances are STALKING THE GIANT by Victoria Leigh (based on "Jack and the Beanstalk"), DRAGON'S EDEN by Glenna McReynolds (based on "Adam and Eve"), HOT SOUTHERN NIGHTS by Patt Bucheister (based on "Little Red Riding Hood"), and CAN'T STOP LOVING YOU by Peggy Webb (based on *Taming of the Shrew*). Each book is available in libraries. Please be sure to list the similarities found below the title of the romance(s) read. Also, for use by the judges in case of a tie, write an essay of 150 words or less stating why you like to read LOVESWEPT romances. Once you've finished your list and your essay, mail your entry to: LOVESWEPT'S TREASURED TALES III CONTEST, Dept. BdG, Bantam Books, 1540 Broadway, New York, NY 10036.

2. PRIZES (3): All three (3) winners will receive a six (6) months' subscription to the LOVESWEPT Book Club and twenty-one (21) autographed books. Each winner will also be featured in a one-page profile that will appear in the back of Bantam Books' LOVESWEPT'S TREASURED TALES IV romances, scheduled for publication in February 1996. (Approximate retail value: $200.00)

3. Contest entries must be postmarked and received by March 31, 1995, and all entrants must be 21 or older on the date of entry. The author of each romance featured in LOVESWEPT'S TREASURED TALES III has provided a list of the similarities between her romance and the classic story it is based on. Entrants need not read all four TREASURED TALES III romances to enter, but the more they read, the more similarities they are likely to find. The entries submitted will be judged by members of the LOVESWEPT Editorial Staff, who will first count up the number of similarities each entrant identified, then compare the similarities found by the entrants who identified the most with the similarities listed by the author of the romance or romances read by those entrants and select the three entrants who correctly identified the greatest number of similarities. If more than three entrants correctly identify the greatest number, the judges will read the essays submitted by each potential winner in order to break the tie and select the entrants who submitted the best essays as the prize winners. The essays will be judged on the basis of the originality, creativity, thoughtfulness, and writing ability shown. All of the judges' decisions are final and binding. All essays must be original. Entries become the property of Bantam Books and will not be returned. Bantam Books is not responsible for incomplete or lost or misdirected entries.

4. Winners will be notified by mail on or about June 15, 1995. Winners have 30 days from the date of notice in which to claim their prize or an alternate winner will be chosen. Odds of winning are dependent on the number of entries received. Prizes are non-transferable and no substitutions are allowed. Winners may be required to execute an Affidavit Of Eligibility And Promotional Release supplied by Bantam Books and will need to supply a photograph of themselves for inclusion in the one-page profile of each winner. Entering the Contest constitutes permission for use of the winner's name, address (city and state), photograph, biographical profile, and Contest essay for publicity and promotional purposes, with no additional compensation.

5. Employees of Bantam Books, Bantam Doubleday Dell Publishing Group, Inc., their subsidiaries and affiliates, and their immediate family members are not eligible to enter. This Contest is open to residents of the U.S. and Canada, excluding the Province of Quebec, and is void wherever prohibited or restricted by law. Taxes, if any, are the winner's sole responsibility.

6. For a list of the winners, send a self-addressed, stamped envelope entirely separate from your entry to LOVESWEPT'S TREASURED TALES III CONTEST WINNERS LIST, Dept. BdG, Bantam Books, 1540 Broadway, New York, NY 10036. The list will be available after August 1, 1995.

THE EDITOR'S CORNER

With March comes gray, rainy days and long, cold nights, but here at LOVESWEPT things are really heating up! The four terrific romances we have in store for you are full of emotion, humor, and passion, with sexy heroes and dazzling heroines you'll never forget. So get ready to treat yourself with next month's LOVESWEPTS—they'll definitely put you in the mood for spring.

Starting things off is the delightfully unique Olivia Rupprecht with **PISTOL IN HIS POCKET**, LOVESWEPT #730. Lori Morgan might dare to believe in a miracle, that a man trapped for decades in a glacier can be revived, but she knows she has no business falling in love with the rough-hewn hunk! Yet when Noble Zhivago draws a breath in her bathtub, she feels reckless enough to respond to the dark stranger who seizes her lips and pulls her into the water. Wooed with passion and purpose by a magnificent warrior who tantalizes her senses, Lori must admit to adoring a man with a dangerous past. Olivia delivers both sizzling sensuality and heartbreaking emotion in this uninhibited romp.

The wonderfully talented Janis Reams Hudson's hero is **CAUGHT IN THE ACT**, LOVESWEPT #731. Betrayed, bleeding, and on the run, Trace Youngblood needs a hiding place—but will Lillian Roberts be his downfall, or his deliverance? The feisty teacher probably believes he is guilty as sin, but he needs her help to clear his name. Drawn to the rugged agent who embodies her secret yearnings, Lillian trusts him with her life, but is afraid she won't escape with her heart. Funny and wild, playful and explosive, smart and sexy, this is definitely another winner from Janis.

Rising star Donna Kauffman offers a captivating heart-stopper with **WILD RAIN**, LOVESWEPT #732. Jillian Bonner insists she isn't leaving, no matter how fierce the tempest headed her way, but Reese Braedon has a job to do—even if it means tossing the sweet spitfire over his shoulder and carrying her off! When the storm traps them together, the sparks that flash between them threaten spontaneous combustion. But once he brands her with the fire of his deepest need, she might never let him go. With a hero as wild and unpredictable as a hurricane, and a heroine who matches him in courage, will, and humor, Donna delivers a tale of outlaws who'd risk anything for passion—and each other.

Last, but never least, is the ever-popular Judy Gill with **SIREN SONG**, LOVESWEPT #733. Returning after fifteen years to the isolated beach where orca whales come to play, Don Jacobs once more feels seduced—by the place, and by memories of a young girl who'd offered him her innocence, a gift he'd hungered for but had to refuse. Tracy Maxwell still bewitches him, but is this beguiling woman of secrets finally free to surrender her heart? This evocative story explores the sweet mystery of longing and passion as only Judy Gill can.

Happy reading!

With warmest wishes,

Beth de Guzman

Senior Editor

P.S. Don't miss the women's novels coming your way in March: **NIGHT SINS**, the first Bantam hardcover by bestselling author Tami Hoag is an electrifying, heart-pounding tale of romantic suspense; **THE FOREVER TREE** by Rosanne Bittner is an epic, romantic saga of California and the courageous men and women who built their dreams out of redwood timber in the bestselling western tradition of Louis L'Amour; **MY GUARDIAN ANGEL** is an enchanting collection of romantic stories featuring a "guardian angel" theme from some of Bantam's finest romance authors, including Kay Hooper, Elizabeth Thornton, Susan Krinard, and Sandra Chastain; **PAGAN BRIDE** by Tamara Leigh is a wonderful historical romance in the bestselling tradition of Julie Garwood and Teresa Medeiros. We'll be giving you a sneak peek at these terrific books in next month's LOVESWEPTs. And immediately following this page, look for a preview of the exciting romances from Bantam that are *available now!*

Don't miss these irresistible books by
your favorite Bantam authors

On sale in January:

VALENTINE
by Jane Feather

PRINCE OF DREAMS
by Susan Krinard

FIRST LOVES
by Jean Stone

From the beguiling, bestselling author of
Vixen and *Velvet* comes a tale brimming
with intrigue and passion

VALENTINE
BY
Jane Feather

"An author to treasure."
—*Romantic Times*

*A quirk of fate has made Sylvester Gilbraith the heir of his
sworn enemy, the earl of Stoneridge. But there's a catch: to
claim his inheritance he has to marry one of the earl's four
granddaughters. The magnetically handsome nobleman
has no choice but to comply with the terms of the will, yet
when he descends on Stoneridge Manor prepared to charm
his way into a fortune, he finds that the lady who intrigues
him most has no intention of becoming his bride. Madden-
ingly beautiful and utterly impossible, Theodora Belmont
refuses to admit to the chemistry between them, even when
she's passionately locked in his embrace. Yet soon the day
will come when the raven-haired vixen will give anything
to be Sylvester's bride and risk everything to defend his
honor . . . and his life.*

"You take one step closer, my lord, and you'll go
down those stairs on your back," Theo said. "And
with any luck you'll break your neck in the process."

Sylvester shook his head. "I don't deny your skill,
but mine is as good, and I have the advantage of size

and strength." He saw the acknowledgment leap into her eyes, but her position didn't change.

"Let's have done with this," he said sharply. "I'm prepared to forget that silly business by the stream."

"Oh, are you, my lord? How very generous of you. As I recall, you were not the one insulted."

"As I recall, you, cousin, were making game of me. Now, come downstairs. I wish you to ride around the estate with me."

"You wish me to do *what*?" Theo stared at him, her eyes incredulous.

"I understand from your mother that you've had the management of the estate for the last three years," he said impatiently, as if his request were the most natural imaginable. "You're the obvious person to show me around."

"You have windmills in your head, sir. I wouldn't give you the time of day!" Theo swung on her heel and made to continue up the stairs.

"You rag-mannered hoyden!" Sylvester exclaimed. "We may have started on the wrong foot, but there's no excuse for such incivility." He sprang after her, catching her around the waist.

She spun, one leg flashing in a high kick aimed at his chest, but as he'd warned her, this time he was ready for her. Twisting, he caught her body across his thighs, swinging a leg over hers, clamping them in a scissors grip between his knees.

"Now, yield!" he gritted through his teeth, adjusting his grip against the sinuous working of her muscles as she fought to free herself.

Theo went suddenly still, her body limp against him. Instinctively he relaxed his grip and the next instant she was free, bounding up the next flight of stairs.

Sylvester went after her, no longer capable of cool

reasoning. A primitive battle was raging and he knew only that he wasn't going to lose it. No matter that it was undignified and totally inappropriate.

Theo raced down the long corridor, hearing his booted feet pounding behind her in time with her thundering heart. She didn't know whether her heart was speeding with fear or exhilaration; she didn't seem capable of rational, coherent thought.

His breath was on the back of her neck as she wrenched open the door of her bedroom and leaped inside, but his foot went in the gap as she tried to slam the door shut. She leaned on the door with all her weight, but Sylvester put his shoulder against the outside and heaved. Theo went reeling into the room and the door swung wide.

Sylvester stepped inside, kicking the door shut behind him.

"Very well," Theo said breathlessly. "If you wish it, I'll apologize for being uncivil. I shouldn't have said what I did just now."

"For once we're in agreement," he remarked, coming toward her. Theo cast a wild look around the room. In a minute she was going to be backed up against the armoire and she didn't have too many tricks left.

Sylvester reached out and seized the long, thick rope of hair hanging down her back. He twisted it around his wrist, reeling her in like a fish until her face was on a level with his shoulder.

He examined her countenance as if he was seeing it for the first time. Her eyes had darkened and he could read the sparking challenge in their depths; a flush of exertion and emotion lay beneath the golden brown of her complexion and her lips were slightly parted, as if she was about to launch into another of her tirades.

To prevent such a thing, he tightened his grip on her plait, bringing her face hard against his shoulder, and kissed her.

Theo was so startled that she forgot about resistance for a split second, and in that second discovered that she was enjoying the sensation. Her lips parted beneath the probing thrust of his tongue and her own tongue touched his, at first tentatively, then with increasing confidence. She inhaled the scent of his skin, a sun-warmed earthy smell that was new to her. His mouth tasted of wine. His body was hard-muscled against her own, and when she stirred slightly she became startlingly aware of a stiffness in his loins. Instinctively she pressed her lower body against his.

Sylvester drew back abruptly, his eyes hooded as he looked down into her intent face. "I'll be damned," he muttered. "How many men have you kissed?"

"None," she said truthfully. Her anger had vanished completely, surprise and curiosity in its place. She wasn't even sure whether she still disliked him.

"I'll be damned," he said again, a slight smile tugging at the corners of his mouth, little glints of amusement sparking in the gray eyes. "I doubt you'll be a restful wife, cousin, but I'll lay odds you'll be full of surprises."

Theo remembered that she *did* dislike him . . . intensely. She twitched her plait out of his slackened grip and stepped back. "I fail to see what business that is of yours, Lord Stoneridge."

"Ah, yes, I was forgetting we haven't discussed this as yet," he said, folding his arms, regarding her with deepening amusement. "We're going to be married, you and I."

PRINCE OF DREAMS
BY
Susan Krinard

For a moment the woman across the table was no more than a jumble of colors and heat and flaring life force. Nicholas struggled to focus on her face, on her stubborn, intelligent eyes.

He said the first thing that came into his head. "Do you have a first name, Dr. Ransom?"

She blinked at him, caught off guard and resentful of it. "I don't see what that has to do with Keely or where she is, Mr. Gale. That's all I'm interested in at the moment. If you—"

"Then we're back to where we started, Dr. Ransom. As it happens, I share your concern for Keely." He lost his train of thought for a moment, looking at the woman with her brittle control and overwhelming aura. He could almost hear the singing of her life force in the three feet of space between them.

He nearly reached out to touch her. Just to see what she would feel like, if that psychic energy would flow into him with so simple a joining.

He stopped his hand halfway across the table and clenched it carefully. She had never seen him move.

"What *is* your business, Mr. Gale?" she asked. The antagonism in her voice had grown muted, and there was a flicker of uncertainty in her eyes.

"I have many varied . . . interests," he said honestly. He smiled, and for a moment he loosed a tiny part of his hunter's power.

She stared at him and lifted a small hand to run her fingers through her short brown hair, effectively disordering the loose curls. That simple act affected Nicholas with unexpected power. He felt his groin tighten, a physical response he had learned to control and ignore long ago.

When was the last time? he asked himself. The last time he had lain with a woman, joined with her physically, taken some part of what he needed in the act of love?

Before he could blunt the thought, his imagination slipped its bonds, conjuring up an image of this woman, her aura ablaze, naked and willing and fully conscious beneath him. Knowing what he was, giving and receiving without fear. . . .

"Diana."

"What?" Reality ripped through Nicholas, dispelling the erotic, impossible vision.

"My first name is Diana," she murmured.

Her face was flushed, as if she had seen the lust in his eyes. She was an attractive woman. Mortal men would pursue her, even blind to her aura as they must be. Did she look at him and observe only another predictable male response to be dissected with an analyst's detachment?

His hungers were not so simple. He would have given the world to make them so.

"Diana," he repeated softly. "Huntress, and goddess of the moon."

She wet her lips. "It's getting late, Mr. Gale—"

"*My* first name is Nicholas."

"Nicholas," she echoed, as if by rote. "I'll be making a few more inquiries about Keely. If you were serious about being concerned for her—"

"I was."

Diana twisted around in her chair and lifted a small, neat purse. "Here," she said, slipping a card from a silver case. "This is where you can reach me if you should hear from her."

Nicholas took the card and examined the utilitarian printing. *Diana Ransom, Ph.D. Licensed Psychologist. Individual psychotherapy. Treatment of depression, anxiety, phobias, and related sleep disorders.*

Sleep disorders. Nicholas almost smiled at the irony of it. She could never cure his particular disorder. He looked up at her. "If you need to talk to me again, I'm here most nights."

"Then you don't plan to leave town in the next few days?" she asked with a touch of her former hostility.

His gaze was steady. "No, Diana. I'll make a few inquiries of my own."

They stared at each other. *Diana.* Was she a child of the night, as her name implied? Did she dream vivid dreams that he could enter as he could never enter her body? Or was she part of the sane and solid world of daylight, oblivious to the untapped power that sang in her aura like a beacon in darkness?

She was the first to look away. Hitching the strap of her purse higher on her shoulder, she rose. "Then I'll be going." She hesitated, slanting a look back at him with narrowed blue eyes. "Perhaps we'll see each other again . . . Nicholas."

He watched her walk away and up the stairs. Her words had held a warning. No promise, no hint of flirtation. With even a little effort he could have won her over. He could have learned more about her, perhaps enough to determine if she would be a suitable candidate to serve his needs. One glimpse of her aura was enough to tempt him almost beyond reason.

But she had affected him too deeply. He could not afford even the slightest loss of control with his dreamers. Emotional detachment was a matter of survival—his and that of the women he touched by night.

Diana Ransom was something almost beyond his experience—.

Although he would never sample the promise behind Diana Ransom's unremarkable façade, would never slip into her dreams and skim the abundance of energy that burned beneath her skin. . . .

As he had done a thousand times before, Nicholas schooled himself to detachment and consigned hope and memory to their familiar prisons. If he arranged matters correctly, he need never see Diana Ransom again.

What if you could go back and rediscover
the magic . . . ?

FIRST LOVES
BY
Jean Stone

*For every woman there is a first love, the love she never
forgets. You always wonder what would have happened,
what might have been. Here is a novel of three women
with the courage to go back . . . but could they recover
the magic they left behind?*

"Men," Alissa said. "They really are scum, you
know."

"Maybe it's partly our fault," Meg replied quietly.

"Are you nuts?" Alissa asked. "Besides, how
would you know? You're not even married." She took
a sip of wine. "Bet you have a boyfriend, though.
Some equally successful power attorney, perhaps? Or
maybe that private investigator? What was his
name?"

"His name is Danny. And no, he's only a friend. A
good friend. But right now, there's no one special in
my life."

Alissa set down her glass. "See? If someone as
beautiful and clever and smart as you doesn't have a
boyfriend, it proves they're all scum. I rest my case."

Though she knew Alissa's words could be considered a compliment, Meg suddenly found old feelings
resurfacing, the feelings of being the kid with no fa-

ther, the one who was different, inadequate. "I've had a lot of boyfriends—men friends," she stuttered.

"But how about relationships?" Alissa pressed. "*Real* relationships?"

In her mind Meg saw his face, his eyes, his lips. She felt his touch. "Once," she replied quietly, "a long time ago."

Alissa leaned back in her chair. "Yeah, I guess you could say I had one once, too. But it sure as shit wasn't with my husband. It was before him." She drained her glass and poured another. "God, it was good."

Meg was relieved to have the focus of the conversation off herself. "What happened?"

"His name was Jay. Jay Stockwell. Our parents had summer homes next to each other."

"You were childhood sweethearts?" Zoe asked, then added wistfully, "I think they're the best. Everyone involved is so innocent."

Alissa shook her head. "This wasn't innocence. It was love. Real love."

They grew quiet. Meg thought of Steven Riley, about their affair. That was love. Real love. But it was years ago. A lifetime ago.

The waiter arrived and set their dinners on the red paper placemats. Meg stared at the cheeseburger. Suddenly she had no appetite.

After he left, Zoe spoke. "What is real love, anyway? How do you know? William took good care of me and of Scott. But I can't honestly say I loved him. Not like I'd loved the boy back home."

"Ah," Alissa said, "the boy back home. For me, that was Jay. The trouble was, he didn't want to stay home. He had things to do, a world to save."

"Where did he go?"

Meg was glad Zoe was keeping Alissa talking. She

could feel herself sliding into the lonely depression of thoughts of Steven. She could feel her walls closing around her, her need to escape into herself. For some reason she thought about the cat she'd had then—a gray tiger named Socrates. For the longest time after Steven was gone she'd closed Socrates out of her bedroom. She'd not been able to stand hearing him purr; the sound was too close to the soft snores of Steven beside her, at peace in his slumber after their lovemaking.

"First, Jay went to San Francisco," Alissa was saying, and Meg snapped back to the present. "It was in the early seventies. He'd been deferred from the draft. From Vietnam."

"Was he sick?" Zoe asked.

"No," Alissa said. "He was rich. Rich boys didn't have to go. Jay's family owned—and still do—a megabroadcast conglomerate. TV stations. Radio stations. All over the country. Jay loved broadcasting, but not business. He was a born journalist." She pushed the plate with her untouched cheeseburger and fries aside. "When he went to San Francisco, he gave his family the finger."

"And you never saw him again?" Zoe asked.

Alissa laughed. "Never saw him again? Darling," she said, as she took another sip of wine, "I went with him."

"You went with him?" Even Meg was surprised at this. She couldn't picture Alissa following anyone, anywhere.

"I was eighteen. Love seemed more important than trust funds or appearances or social standing."

"So what happened?" Zoe asked.

She shrugged. "I realized I was wrong."

The women were quiet. Meg felt sorry for Alissa. Something in the eyes of this tiny, busy, aggressive little blonde now spelled sorrow. Sorrow for a life gone by. Sorrow for love relinquished. She knew the feeling only too well.

"God, he was handsome," Alissa said. "He still is."

"Still is?" Zoe asked. "You mean you still see him?"

Alissa shook her head. "I left him standing at the corner of Haight and Ashbury. It seemed appropriate at the time. He was working for one of those liberal underground newspapers. I went home to Atlanta, married Robert, had the kids. Then one day I turned on the TV and there he was. Reporting from Cairo."

"So he went back into broadcasting," Zoe said.

"Full steam ahead, apparently. Delivering stories on the oppressed peoples of the world. Over the years I've seen him standing against backdrops in Lebanon, Ethiopia, Iraq, you name it. He was on the air for days during that Tiananmen Square thing in China or wherever that is."

"Oh," Zoe said, "Jay Stockwell. Sure. I've seen him, too. His stories have real sensitivity."

Alissa shrugged. "I never paid much attention to his stories. I was too busy looking at him. Wondering."

Zoe picked at her scallops, then set down her fork. "Wondering what would have happened if you'd stayed together?"

"Sure. Haven't you ever done that? Wondered about your boy back home?"

"You mean, the man I could have married?" Zoe asked.

"Or should have," Alissa said.

Should have, Meg thought. Should I have? Could I have?

"Sure I've wondered about him," Zoe said. "All the time."

"What about you, Meg? What about your one and only? Don't you ever wonder how your life would have been different. How it would have been better?"

Meg silently wished she could say, "No. My life wouldn't have been better. It would have been worse. And besides, my life is just fine the way it is." But she couldn't seem to say anything. She couldn't seem to lie.

There was silence around the table. Meg looked at Zoe, who was watching Alissa. Meg turned to Alissa, just in time to see her quickly wipe a lone tear from her cheek. Alissa caught Meg's eye and quickly cleared her throat. Then she raised her glass toward them both. "I think we should find them," Alissa said. "I think we should find the men we once loved, and show them what they've missed."

And don't miss these fabulous romances
from Bantam Books,
on sale in February:

NIGHT SINS
Available in hardcover
by the nationally bestselling author

Tami Hoag

THE FOREVER TREE
by the award-winning

Rosanne Bittner

PAGAN BRIDE
by the highly acclaimed

Tamara Leigh

"MY GUARDIAN ANGEL"
anthology featuring:

**Sandra Chastain   Kay Hooper
Susan Krinard   Karyn Monk
Elizabeth Thornton**